Changeling Nine Changeling Nine Changelin

Series editor: Allan Cameron

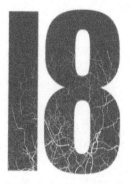

PAULS BANKOVSKIS

Translated from Latvian by **Ieva Lešinska**

VAGABOND VOICES

GLASGOW

Original Latvian text first published in 2014 as *18*
© Pauls Bankovskis

Translation copyright © Vagabond Voices Publishing Ltd.

First published in September 2017 by
Vagabond Voices Publishing Ltd.,
Glasgow,
Scotland.

ISBN 978-1-908251-78-7

The author's right to be identified as author of this book under the
Copyright, Designs and Patents Act 1988 has been asserted.

Printed and bound in Poland

Cover design by Mark Mechan

Typeset by Park Productions

The publisher acknowledges subsidy towards
the translation, publication and marketing from
the Latvian Ministry of Culture and the
Latvian Writers' Union

Kultūras ministrija

For further information on Vagabond Voices, see the website,
www.vagabondvoices.co.uk

In the distance, far away,
Something dazzling they beheld –
Straightaway they steered the ship
To the very place where stood
The Diamond Mountain, fine and tall.
Shadows veiled the noble mount,
And the summit brightly shone,
Covered by the sun's rays,
Fashioned from gold and jewels.
The helmsman brought the mighty vessel,
To a halt and every man rushed ashore,
Keen to know the nature of
What it was that shone so bright.
Bearslayer told them to stay put,
Yet the one who climbed to the very top
stood there and called out,
"Oh my, it's beautiful up here!"
And then, as if on the wings of wind,
He was snatched for ever from human sight.

Andrejs Pumpurs, *Bearslayer*

I got a
Baby's brain and an old man's heart
Took eighteen years to get this far.

Alice Cooper, "I'm Eighteen"

When benevolent mercy bestows gifts upon this land,
It wishes new joys for its own glory to be bestowed upon
this land,
It wishes new light and its grandeur to reveal to this land,
To reveal all that is pure and bright to this land,
To remove all that is evil and artful from this land,
To remove all that is dirty and sick from this land,
To remove the false idols and false temples from this
land…

Henrici Chronicon

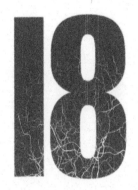

I. OVERCOAT

Whenever we go to the country, we start to clean, and when we leave, all is order and cleanliness. Yet when we return, we have this irresistible urge to straighten everything out even more than before.

Of course, rodents have left their droppings here and there; spiders have woven their webs; there are a few dead flies on the windowsills; the hornets' nest in the corner of the attic window is already empty and eroded; the bird's nest behind the balcony railing has been abandoned; everywhere, there are the brown crumbs from oak blossoms, as well as stalks, panicles and pollen of various flowers, grasses and tree blossoms. A mouse that died of starvation is found in the rubbish bin, along with the empty pupae of flies lying next to the desiccated body. On the floor, there may be a forgotten Lego piece or two, waiting for a barefoot adult to step on it, and then there are things, things, things – all sorts of objects that have been put aside year after year, because they "may come in handy" or have been taken to the country on purpose, as they're "no longer of any use in the city but good enough for the country". So the first three days are spent on straightening out and cleaning the house, instead of cutting grass, sawing off dead branches, levelling the patches of soil dug up by moles or wild hogs, or stacking wood.

A woodsman once lived here. Originally it was a squat little house with a couple of rooms built on the hump of a pre-historic dune. Only after many years, the change of owner-ship and death of the woodsman, did it acquire additional rooms and new histories, verandas, attic constructions and city amenities. The woodsman, just like his father, was said to have had his eccentricities: from time to time, each man had been beset by what in their family was called a "teeter-totter". On such occasions, they would leave the house and stay in voluntary confinement in an underground bunker built for this purpose in the forest.

What the house looked like in the woodsman's time, no one can really say any more. You get the basic idea from other buildings scattered throughout the village that have been all but abandoned by the natives: they have a simple, almost square layout, with a couple of rooms and a kitchen. We may have seen the woodsman's house in its original state at the Liv Festival in the local cultural centre. There was a photo exhibition in its lobby, and one of the pictures seemed to feature our house. It was almost half the size, but the setting was exactly as it is now: the rowan in front of the door, an oak by the gable and another slightly further off. Two people were standing by the door to the house, and a third was sitting on a stool. In old photographs, you're usually struck by the sharpness and depth of the image; sometimes, the most incredible details can be detected in them, but this particular photo-graph was very blurry – people's faces were so smudgy, it was impossible to determine their age or sex. Images from the past, wrapped in a white, fuzzy mist, were staring back at us from the time immortalised in the picture and from the front of our own house.

The trash bags were filling rapidly, and the list of things that should be bought on the next trip to town grew with equal rapidity. There were things we threw away, but there were others we'd been missing all the while.

"Just don't throw away Grandpa's overcoat," was the instruction issued during this process.

His overcoat should by no means end up in the trash, it was decided.

"We should definitely keep Grandpa's overcoat."

And the overcoat was on its way back to the wardrobe; it only remained to check its pockets. In one of them, there was something angular, bulky and hard. It was a rough leather case, wrinkled in places, which contained a small black camera. For a moment, I imagined that perhaps it had belonged to Grandpa, but that was not possible. It was a Lumix digital camera, and at the time they started making them and it could be bought, Grandpa, in all likelihood, no longer took pictures or even went to the country. The battery was dead, the camera would not turn on, and the only clue to its provenance could be provided by the memory card. The solution to the mystery had to wait until our return to the city and a computer.

Back in the city, we were impatient to pop the memory card into the computer, though we were almost certain that we wouldn't find anything special there – probably just some pictures taken in the dark by a summer solstice bonfire, or perhaps a seascape. For the most part, we were right: the pictures weren't terribly interesting, but neither were they ordinary shots of the countryside, everyday life or festive occasions.

Photograph 1

At a first glance it seemed that only a forest was pictured – and not even a forest, just shrubbery and a mass of undergrowth. There was almost no colour, the picture was nearly black and white; it must've been taken either on a day with dark clouds or at the twilight hour of an overcast day. The trees and shrubs formed a black, almost opaque wall on either side, and only in the middle of the picture did the wall thin out and lower to reveal a firebreak overgrown with small shrubs. There were also two power poles.

The place seemed familiar, but we scrutinised it for quite a while before finally figuring out where it was, and from what angle the unknown photographer had captured it.

Looking at the photograph more closely we noticed a tiny triangle behind the tangle of branches on the left side. It was the gable of our house.

Why anyone would have taken that photograph or decided upon that viewpoint was a mystery: it was no more than an impenetrable thicket alternating with persistently waterlogged swampland. No mushrooms, berries or anything else worthwhile would ever have been found there. A little to the right of the tiny triangle marking out our house, between a power pole and the other wall of shrubbery, we could spy something that looked like a small white human figure, but it may have been just some optical illusion or technical defect. We zoomed in as much as possible, yet all we could see was a mess of grey, white and black specks. We agreed to try and find that vantage point on our next visit to the countryside.

Photograph 2

There was a building in the photo. Of course, buildings tend to resemble one another, but the arrangement of trees around it, particularly the big oak, made it obvious that it was the shed in the corner of our yard. And yet it wasn't exactly like the one we knew so well. Its entire wall was covered by small splotches; only by enlarging the image would it have been possible to tell that they were shoes somehow attached to the wall. It looked as though no two were alike; they could have been shoes and sandals for the same foot. Oh, and one door to the shed was open – the door leading to a space we call "the workshop" because Grandpa once set one up in there, complete with a carpenter's bench and tools. He even installed electricity. There seemed to be a tall person in light-coloured dress standing there in the darkness behind the open door, but it could also have been a sunbeam entering the workshop through a side window.

Photograph 3

There was something mysterious in this picture too. It showed a path in the woods on a sunny day, and could have been taken during any season except winter. The location was also ambiguous, as pine forests and sandy, mossy roads are common features throughout that part of our country. It could well have been the track of the old narrow-gauge or one of the roads created by Soviet tanks on the other bank of the river, next to the former shooting range.

What was striking about this photograph was the wooden building – or more accurately, the shack. On the side of the road, there were four posts dug into the ground, and several cross-beams placed on top of them, from which remnants of the roof dangled. Not much remained of the walls. It was possible that at one end the shack had been burnt. Inside, the floor was cluttered with all kinds of junk, including a flattened mattress.

Only after perusing this photo several times did we notice a silhouette in the distance, behind a pine leaning to the wind. Although it was blurry and resembled the snowman or yeti from that infamous "documentary" footage, it was clearly a human or human-like creature, and not a moose, elk or deer.

Photograph 4

Another familiar place. That big oak tree must have been the one that still stood in our backyard, yet against its trunk was some strange construction resembling a house on stilts. Its purpose was impossible to discern. Was it for birdwatching or was it a hunter's hide? It felt futile to waste time guessing, as the shack was certainly no longer there.

We would have paid little attention to this picture if it hadn't been for the mysterious silhouette which reappeared here as well. Of course, we'd allowed for the possibility that we might start to perceive it in pictures where it wasn't present, but this was not the case. Far off, at the edge of the woods, concealed by the shadows cast by the big aspens, someone was standing by the little gate. And he seemed to be looking our way.

Photograph 5

Only the ground. The forest floor appeared to be what interested the photographer: a few clusters of blueberries, heather, possibly a cowberry here and there. Some scattered pine needles, pine cones and slivers of bark. Moss. At the centre of the photograph, there was a black square. Since the picture was not taken from above, the square was seen in perspective; the similarity with Malevich's painting was purely intuitive. The square was a hole dug in the forest floor. The precise form invited speculation that the hole had been reinforced and, in all likelihood, represented an entrance to some underground space. It could have been an abandoned cellar or something to do with the Soviet army. In the depth of this opening, in the dark, something greyish and bulky could be discerned. Possibly as a result of looking at the other pictures, one felt the temptation to see in this blurry outline something that could qualify as a living being.

Photograph 6

Yet another familiar place: a shack overgrown with long grass, alders, untrimmed apple trees and berry bushes half-way to the sea. It was impossible to get to the sea that way because our neighbours were dredging the ditch, creating huge piles of earth and blocking the route to the water. At one time there must have been a substantial house – with a barn, shed and other outbuildings. The ruined shack was visible not so long ago. We refer to this place as the

Doctor's House. A doctor is said to have lived there once. When we snuck inside one day to investigate, we found some dusty but still full medicine bottles and mouldy medical handbooks.

Photograph 7

A view from the village cemetery. The photo must have been taken in the evening, against the light. The sun is already behind the trees and the lighthouse. There are black outlines of tree trunks and shadows, contrasting slices of light against a simple grave overgrown with tiny plants. There is no cross and no headstone.

Video 1

The last file preserved on the memory card was a short video fragment. It had been shot in insufficient lighting on a windy evening. Almost nothing could be picked out in the grey-black grainy footage. Gusts of wind blowing right into the camera microphone were audible, as was the rustling of branches. If you watched it in slow motion, possibly a fragment of the fence around the house could be seen in the darkness, but it was not clear whether the cameraman was standing on the inside or on the outside of the fence. At first it seemed that in the thirty-three-second recording there was no movement, but if you watched it several times you slowly began to feel that the cameraman himself was moving forward, as branches squeaked and leaves rustled. During the last tenth of a second, something flashed brightly in the centre of the frame, yet the source of light could not be discerned.

II. JOURNAL

20 August 1917

"To hope!" Tidriķis made a toast, raising his glass of cut crystal. The first of the three bottles remaining from the pre-war time was close to empty.

"To hell with it!" Alberts replied, clinking energetically with Tidriķis.

"Hope is the comfort of fools!" I joined in. The night before, we drank to the memory of the ill-fated dream of Latvia's statehood and independence. And the more bubbly we drank, the greater our grim conviction became that we would turn out to be right. It's all over. Done for. We Latvians simply aimed too high. We are doomed. We cannot shake off either the Russians or the Germans and be free. If one lot are gone, they will be replaced by others, and we'll continue to have no say in our own destiny.

If at the beginning of the year, revolution still brought some hope, now it has vanished. What use are these revolutionaries if their own nation has no faith in them? And how can the nation believe in them if they look down their noses on the nation? All this revolution achieved is greater calamity than the one brought by democracy. If there had not been this damn revolution, the Bolsheviks would not be free to stir up trouble and get our army to the point where it is now.

The army can't even defend Riga. With shame and sorrow, we have to run from our city, possibly forever. At six o'clock in the evening, the order to retreat was issued.

"Let's not leave champagne for the Germans!" Alberts said. But I had to think about what we'd have to leave behind, for you can't take everything with you. The Germans had started an attack on Riga and were advancing rapidly, but the army was losing all ability and will to resist. The soldiers are spoiled, emboldened by the Bolsheviks and lazy. They treat us, the officers, as the real enemy. But you can't shoot everyone just to intimidate the others. After all, they are our own boys, our own men. Yet they stare at you as if you were their farm foreman; they ignore your orders and want to fraternise with the Germans. Apparently, they even threw rocks at General Goppers when he came to try to straighten them out. How can one think of Latvia if you can't even recognise your fellow Latvians? Where has all the zeal gone that made us establish our own regiments of riflemen and issue the call, "Forward under Latvian flags for the future of Latvia!" All those Bolsheviks, congress-goers, rally-goers, Mensheviks, socialists and God only knows who else. Everyone imagines himself to be the best and the wisest while all the rest are enemies, saboteurs and fools. "Hard times in the land of our fathers, it's up to the sons to help?" Hell, no. We don't deserve a state. Trophy pickers, daydreamers, windbags.

21 August

It had rained during the night, and the sunny, crisp morning signalled autumn. The fresh, cool air did wonders for the fog in my brain and it soon dissipated. Although it was still very early, there was much activity in our yard on Alexander Street. The old Neļķises from the small house at the back of the yard kept tugging at their two cows, which they were apparently moving to a safer place. One cow seemed ready to go, but the other was resisting. Their boy Leopolds was trying to catch the chickens that had scattered all over the yard. The noise of war was not heard, and it all looked like a tableau from a country fair. In some neighbouring yard a rooster crowed. In the middle of the yard by the horse chestnut a horse ate from a sack of oats. That must have been the cart of the Šteinbergs family from the front building – I recognised their chest of drawers and some other things that were tied to the top of the load.

There was much activity on the street as well, mostly in one direction: away from Riga. There were army units intermingled with civilians – many on foot and all kinds of drivers and riders – in carriages and carts, on horseback, on bicycles. What they all shared was the quantity of stuff they'd taken – that they dragged, lugged and carried, and it almost seemed that what they carried was not really their own, particularly in the soldiers' case. The edible and inedible was looted from what had already been "commandeered" from the city warehouses and "rescued" from citizens' apartments. There were reams of fabric, musical instruments, sacks of flour, furniture, and piles of suits with hams and sausage links on top.

I was caught in this current of people as soon as I'd stepped out of the yard. By the Orthodox Church on the corner of Neva Street I ran into Miss M, whom I was surprised to see striding, in a most determined fashion, in the opposite direction. We were not well acquainted, having seen each other only on a few festive occasions, yet these extreme circumstances seemed to grant me the right not only to greet but also to address her. In truth, she was the first one to speak.

"And where are you off to?" she asked.

Confused, I did not reply right away, but just pulled on the strap of the sack I had over my shoulder with even more determination. The glass of a broken shop window was crunching under the soles of my boots. My sack held all of the belongings I'd chosen to take along: there was nothing of sentimental or luxurious value, just a shaving kit, a clean pair of underwear and a small, worn brochure pamphlet – *The Antichrist* by Nietzsche. I was in the habit of making notes on the edges of its pages, even though I always carry a small notebook with light brown cardboard covers, in which I am presently making this journal entry.

By now I was effectively a deserter, although I was walking with my former battlefield comrades in the same direction. But, as of the previous night, our intentions set us apart. The passing army units were still obeying the orders of their commanding officers – irrespective of whether they remained loyal to the Russian high command or had had their minds turned against it by the Bolsheviks. If anyone asked, I could say that I was about to join my unit in the hussars' barracks by the Church of the Holy Cross – in my pocket I even had papers to that effect. Naturally there was no need to tell any of this to Miss M.

"But of course," seeing my confusion, she found her own answer. "You must follow orders, must you not?"

"Absolutely," I said as resolutely as possible, and asked if she was not going to leave the city herself. "It is no longer safe here," I tried to convince her.

"It's certainly not, now that you are abandoning us," she chuckled. "So long!"

A moment after we said goodbye to each other there was great commotion when a German shell fell right there on Alexander Street, followed by two more. In an instant the street was empty; at the intersection, the water main had been hit and a fountain of water shot up into the air. A building had lost its facade, revealing a dresser, a bed and a painting on one of the remaining walls (a Rozentāls, if I am not mistaken). A crowd soon began to gather. I couldn't forget my brief conversation with M, which bothered me until I reached my first destination. Miss M's political views notwithstanding, she regarded me as a traitor. Her political sympathies were unknown to me at the time, yet her mood was not hard to guess.

Only later, many years later, did I find out that first she had been an active social democrat, and then, after the founding of the Latvian state, she had been arrested for anti-government activities. When the Soviet regime was set up in 1940, she became an active collaborator, only to disappear in Siberia a few years later.

Traitor. Unlike Tidriķis, who had urged us to drink for hope, and the ever-sceptical Alberts, I'd decided to stop my war that very morning – to try and save my own skin. No political or moral ideals, just existence, pure and simple. Wasn't this the main lesson to be learnt from the horrors of war – a lesson taught to us both on the Island of Death and last winter in Tīreļpurvs Bog? Even as you face death in the name of a common goal, you are alone. Alone with your hands turned to icy stone, alone with your stiffened arms stretched out to the heavens and your face a mess of blood, snow and ice. You are alone, entangled in barbed wire and alone with your bayonet drawn on the edge of the German trench.

On that morning, I had no idea that very soon my path would cross those of Tidriķis and Alberts, and then we would become three people completely different from our former selves.

By Šmerlis Forest, my route divided from the general flow of people travelling on foot and on wheels. Leaving and not knowing whether I would ever come back, I wanted to visit my parents and see places dear to me one last time. My mother and father had been managing a small estate on the banks of Lake Ķīšezers. The owners of the estate, Germans, had not been seen there since the beginning of the war, but my parents firmly believed that the place had to be kept in good shape until the moment of their return.

I crossed the railroad and sat down by the small lake of Ozolkalns to smoke a cigarette. I remembered how the sappers of the Fifth Zemgale Latvian Riflemen's battalion used to bring their horses here for a swim. There were moments when the war seemed deceptively distant and unreal.

After a short walk through the forest, the big oak trees and stunning lime trees of the estate came into view.

Autumn smells filled the air: the ground was covered in colourful apples, and heavily laden branches of apple trees were bending the supports beneath them; close by, a variety of plums gleamed in the sun, acorns crunched under my feet, and the bright heads of autumn flowers were leaning over the fence around the flower garden.

A dog barked – it was our good old Bear with his grey muzzle. The rattling of buckets could be heard from the barn, and chickens were clucking – they were kept here out of pity: my mother wouldn't let my father slaughter even the ones that no longer laid eggs, and thus they awaited a natural conclusion to their lives.

I didn't say anything about my decisions, new status or plans to my parents. I didn't want to worry them unnecessarily, although I noticed that they seemed concerned anyway. My father tried to spoil me as usual, offering me coffee again and again, and encouraging me to eat some more, for "they're starving you out there in the trenches." My mother complained that yet again I was only looking in for a moment, that I was always passing through and that there was never a chance to have a good heart-to-heart with me.

As we said our goodbyes, my father wouldn't take no for an answer and poured all kinds of apples into my bag – including the dark red ones with the white flesh, which had been my favourites since childhood. I hugged my mother and wondered again at how thin and small she had become over the years. My father shunned such bodily contact and gave me barely a wave, yet this behaviour was probably in total contradiction to what was happening in his soul, for I spotted tears in his eyes. Then he turned away abruptly and went back to his work. My mother stood under the limes for a long time, following me with her gaze, until I walked out on the road and began marching along the Ķīšezers shoreline towards Jugla.

The experience of leaving or arriving in a city differs greatly according to whether you're on horseback, in a cart, on a train or on foot. The brothers Kaudzīte, Reinis and Matīss are said to have walked all the way to Paris to see the Eiffel Tower. I am sure that what they saw, felt and thought along the way would have been entirely different had they travelled in modern haste – in a carriage or, say, a steamer.

Putting more and more distance between myself and my dear Riga – albeit doing it at the speed not of a steam engine or a horse, but at the rhythm of my own footsteps – I pushed away from all I'd held dear and cherished, and all I considered important in my not-so-long life, each and every time my boots crunched the pebbles on the road. Had I been a passenger of some kind, I probably wouldn't have thought about it so much. The train, carriage, steamer – even a bicycle – would provide the necessary speed of travel; there wouldn't be so much time for such sentiments and they wouldn't have weighed so heavily on my shoulders.

In addition to all the other things it has made unrecognisable or completely destroyed, this war must have changed man's ability to distinguish between speed and slowness, haste and thoroughness. When you look back on the history of warfare, everything depended on speed. When foot soldiers turned out to be too slow, cavalry and the chariot were invented. Man realised that, in order to win in battle, often reckless – not to say monstrous – speeds are required. Firearms, navy, armoured trains, war aeroplanes and dirigibles – they are all attempts to surprise an unprepared adversary, to be quicker than the enemy.

Yet ways of conducting war become dated almost as quickly as ladies' summer fashions. For example, the Dvinsk Fortress was under construction in 1812, when a battle with Napoleon's army took place outside its walls. All the efforts expended on building such fortified structures were wasted, as armies could simply circumvent them. The fortress was never completed. War conducted in this manner was already proving to be too slow.

I suspect that this hankering for speed and the need of an element of surprise in warfare infects us in all other undertakings – both in everyday life as well as in art and culture. People are increasingly and persistently harassed, and therefore become more negligent. Even music, as was obvious at the end of the last century, is becoming ever faster and louder. And there are only a handful of people bothered that the ability to delve into things, observe what is happening around and inside oneself, and contemplate and judge seems to be dwindling equally fast. Various means of transportation, telegraph, telephone, phonograph, cinema and newspapers, which are the instruments of immediacy making every event suddenly available and consumable for our entertainment, are not only reflections of our feverish haste, but also its agents. More, bigger, faster – only that has, and will have in the future – some weight. But they say that you can't run past your own grave. The infamous Titanic was the dark angel of this trend, the whale-like sarcophagus and temple.

This war will also be a horrendous monument to our haste and desire for speed. Hasty, chaotic or contradictory orders; army units abandoned to their fate or misdirected; mysterious disappearances of supplies of ammunition or food: all these have already been paid for in lives and blood, and will continue to do so. I hate to think where the future will take us, as all this rushing around, this headlong velocity and this inability to examine anything in depth will only get worse. We no longer live in Plato's cave, naively enjoying the shadows playing on its walls. That's long gone – we've established a world Plato would find horrifying: it's governed by chimeras, whims, an irrational desire to dwell on the trifling and seek immediate entertainment. Ultimately, it's not knowledge but "artists" who'll predominate here. The ability to get immediately from one part of the world to another, the ability to reach any inhabitant of the world at any given moment – the time will come when these things will be our undoing.

These were more or less my thoughts after I had cautiously crossed the Jugla railway bridge and was walking along the Jugla-Baltezers Canal. If I hadn't noticed a heavy army train lumber over the embankment towards Vidzeme right beside me, and if my mood had been different, I could have forgotten myself and imagined that I was merely on a little stroll around the city's outskirts. Here, real countryside began: well-worked fields, pastures, cattle, and dogs barking somewhere in the distance. I perceived the bridge as the last boundary of the city – beyond it, there was no turning back. "I am burning all my bridges," I thought to myself.

And even if there comes a time when I'll return, Riga won't be the same place I left today. And I too will be another. The thought that it's impossible to return to the same place seems to us as self-evident as the words of the ancient Greek philosopher Heraclitus: "One can never step in the same river twice." It's clear that a river or canal will continue to flow along the same bed (unless it has dried up of course): the Gauja will remain the Gauja, and although you can still step into it, it's not the same water – that water flowed away long ago. We find it pleasing to imagine that time moves forward while space, what surrounds us, is immobile, always available, and awaits us like a painting we've perused countless times on a museum wall – or like a ripe apple on a branch (an apple is the best simile, for now you see one, now you don't). We live confidently in a world in which it seems to be a given that we'll wake in the same bed and room in which we go to sleep, where beyond our front doors the same street or meadow will greet us, trees will be found exactly where they have "always" been, and the people we met yesterday will be the same the day after tomorrow: everything will largely remain unchanged irrespective of the hour, the day or the regular cycle of falling asleep and waking up.

You can pretend not to see it in the ever-increasing haste, but you need only stop, or begin moving at a slightly slower pace, and you'll understand that there are many more things for which you'll never have time, and many more places which you'll never visit or return to, than all that you have already experienced in life.

I was deliberately circumventing the St Petersburg road, and favouring smaller roads where I was less likely to run into the retreating army. There was no need to skulk around. Even then, I must admit that when I was still near Riga, I took to the roadside bushes a few times upon hearing the clatter of hooves behind me.

Thickets of hops had twined themselves around the alders and were blooming with light green, intoxicating flowers. It promised a good harvest. If the barley harvest was equally good this year, farmers could brew a fair amount of strong beer. But it's doubtful that there'll be anyone to do the harvesting, let alone someone wanting to waste barley on beer. I'm not sure if such a time will ever come.

In order not to lose my way, I looked at the map from time to time, but I either knew or could surmise the direction even without it: past both Baltezers Lakes, the big and the small, then along the Gauja-Baltezers Canal to the Gauja, and then upstream along the Gauja towards Garkalne. Past Great Baltezers, and I had to be careful crossing the highway that leads to Neubad. Towards the Vidzeme coast, I came across a stream of refugees with their heavy carts, interspersed here and there with army ones. I could cross only by the bridge that spans the Baltezers Canal, and then I continued on along the shore of Lesser Baltezers where there was less chance of unpleasant surprises. I satisfied my sweet tooth with plums and hazelnuts, which were particularly abundant this year and which I plucked near the Baltezers water facility. By the Alderi Inn I looked back at Baltezers for the last time and then continued towards the Gauja lock along the canal where in peacetime logs were floated down.

Near Garkalne I had an amusing encounter. As I was walking along the forest road I heard a horse-drawn cart slowly draw nearer from behind. Since I did not perceive any danger, I stayed on the road and continued walking. It was quite a surprise when the cart stopped next to me and a familiar voice asked if I needed a ride. It took a while for me to recognise Miss K sitting in the cart. I knew both her brothers quite well from my time at the Polytechnic. Like me, Ernests had been studying engineering and the elder, Pauls, economics. I'd heard that Ernests was wounded.

After politely declining the ride, I asked if Miss K was not afraid to drive like this – all alone, with the war going on – but she replied that there was too much to do on the farm to worry about such things.

"But the Germans will be here soon," I tried to convince her.

"You can't take unharvested fields with you," she said. "It's time to harvest the rye just now, and Father is busy from dawn to dusk. And what would we do with the cattle? Whatever God's design, we'll have to live with it."

Upon saying goodbye she asked me once more if I'd change my mind, and made me promise to stop by their farm should I feel hungry. I thanked her for the invitation, she prodded the horse, I heard the clatter of empty milk cans, and soon the cart disappeared around the bend.

I never met Miss K again.

I've not had a chance to figure out the reason, but people tend to hold on to the mistaken idea that almost any kind of change will bring something better than what's already the case. The line of thought is that if you're dissatisfied with the status quo, change is necessary and will bring about sufficient improvement. In general terms we like to call it progress. Yet history is full of evidence that suggests how erroneous this thinking is. For instance, the tsar's overthrow and the so-called democratic election in February did not bring any benefit or gain; it only increased the chaos and misery, and brought the realisation that the Russian intelligentsia and the rest of the Russian people are two worlds that will never meet. The Bolsheviks think the same way: they too are unhappy with the existing order of things and demand changes, but knowing these people a little, I'm convinced that for the majority of people these changes the Bolsheviks have dreamt up will not make life any better.

Yes, I may be a pessimist, but I know that it's much wiser to be a knowing pessimist than an ignorant optimist who has found shelter in his illusions. "I told you so," says a pessimist when something does not happen exactly as planned, whereas an optimist experiences one disappointment after another. And exactly this – pessimism – is my attitude towards any kind of change and the possible improvement it brings. All of our history – and I mean not only the experience of my people but humanity as a whole – I regard not as constant improvement and progress but as degradation, degeneration, downslide and demise. The ever-increasing haste, speed and quantity – as I already stated, I do not see any achievement in all that. I remember that it says in the book of Revelation that at the end of time the entire world will close like a book. Even though I'm an atheist and believe that God is dead – and this war is certainly the proof – I find in this biblical parable what's lacking in all this talk of revolutions, changes, improvements and progress. Namely, there's no clearly marked point at which a person can finally stop, sit down, draw breath and say: "Enough!"

I remember something I once heard from Tidriķis, I think. A Riga master carpenter was evaluating the masterpieces made by his disciples. One of them, a very scrupulous and dexterous fellow, had made a chair decorated with fine carvings. Each carving was polished and varnished to perfection, however when the old master turned the chair upside down he said to the disciple: "You will never become a master! You overdo it." The disciple had painstakingly polished and varnished even the bottoms of the chair's feet.

Though I used a map and consider myself to be a decent topographer, I managed to lose my way in the forest near Murjāṇi. Apparently I had taken a side road too early and thus I had to walk several miles blindly and probably in the wrong direction. An unnecessarily long time was spent in such wandering, and if this wasn't displeasing enough, I noticed that a seam was unravelling on my right boot, making it wobble slightly and chafe. It was a consolation to end up in a field and spot a steeple with a cross in the distance; a look at the map convinced me that it was the Vangaži Church, which meant that I was once again on the right path.

My relief at regaining the right path was tempered by my uncomfortable boot and the growing concern that I would soon need drinking water. When I was walking beside Baltezers lakes and the canal, the proximity of vast expanses of water must have given me the mistaken impression that there was no need to keep my water bottle full. With the sun rising higher and the heat increasing, I had been emptying it rather quickly. As I re-entered the forest, I couldn't find any sign of a brook or a ditch, but it's a well-known fact that a person need only think of water and, if none is readily available, their feelings of thirst will become much stronger than if they had a full bottle in their knapsack.

There was no longer any question of intelligent contemplation: for three to four miles, I marched like a lifeless automaton until I noticed a tiny farm in the shadowy crescent of the forest – with hindsight it was probably a forester's house. As no dog or people could be seen, I stepped cautiously into the yard. It would have been a disappointment to accidentally run into a small army unit after all this walking. Yet there was no one in the yard either, only in front of the barn an elderly man was doing something by the trough. My sudden appearance startled him, yet he asked no questions. Taking the measure of me from head to foot, he must have come to his own conclusions, but he kept them to himself. I felt – it may have been just me – that his assessment was hardly flattering. My request for water really amused him for some reason; his face suggested he was about to burst out laughing, yet he composed himself.

"Do you have anything for water?" the man asked and even in this question I detected a hint of pulling my leg – he seemed to be convinced that I could not have any vessel.

"Yes, I do," I said and pulled a bottle out of my knapsack.

"The water is good, very good." The man pulled up some water from the well and at that very moment lost all interest in me and returned to chopping up the green forage.

He was right: the water really was extremely tasty, very cold and as if full of tiny, effervescent bubbles. I drank and could not quench my thirst until the cold had made my palate numb. Then I filled my bottle and said goodbye to the old man.

He not only gave no reply but did not so much as glance in my direction, settling for just a gesture with his hand, which I found hurtful. Traitor, deserter, coward, a fugitive and a vagabond – there were only a limited number of descriptions which he might have used to characterise me. Whereas he had grown to be as one with this place on Earth as a deeply rooted oak. He had no intention of bending right or left or going somewhere: his place was here. This house would not exist without him and without the house he would not exist.

It was late afternoon when I came to the Gauja at Murjāni. On the sandy shore, I took off my boots and assessed the damage wrought by the broken boot. When I walked up to the water's edge, intending to sit down and cool my overheated and chafed feet, a large grass snake slithered off a tuft of grass and into the water. Wriggling its body, it swam for a while against the current and then came back ashore. It did not bother me, I did not bother it: we had reached a wordless understanding. There had been lots of rain in the previous days, and the Gauja flowed muddy and brown. I lay down in the grass, looked at the rustling play of willow leaves above my head and tried to work out my impressions of the day so that I could write them down later.

Could it be that I was witnessing something as great and important as the collapse of the Roman Empire? Of course, the demise of ancient Rome was also caused by its "culture". In their sophistication, they had found ways of answering every need and sating every taste or desire. But the barbarians could do without all that and did them in. Above all other things, humans and all that they manage to achieve within their lives are mortal, and only by adopting this approach can we find the history of mankind worthy of consideration. You're born, you grow up, you get old and you die. And nothing remains. The Reformation, the great scientific discoveries, the French Revolution, Enlightenment, the first socialist ideas, this awful war – all that comes upon us is intended to wipe away the old and create something new. And all the while, we pretend to be unaware that the advocates of the new will also disappear into the abyss sooner or later. History doesn't repeat itself by moving in a circle, and time is not a dialectical spiral: we move ever lower and deeper, enduring one circle of Dante's hell after another, and all we can see before us is impenetrable darkness.

I might have fallen asleep on this thought – always supposing it was a thought and not a waking dream. I sat up with a start. It felt as if some unfathomable danger was lurking all around me – that at any moment someone could have emerged from the bushes with the intention of capturing or killing me on the spot. Yet it was only wind bending osier branches and occasionally carrying voices or noises from the nearby Gauja river crossing at Murjāņi. I began to think that it would have been wiser to cross the river at Iļķene where there would have been less traffic, but now it was too late. I had no desire to backtrack all those miles.

I managed to get across the Gauja without incident. There were only refugees from Riga and its outskirts, along with their carts and cattle, crowding around the crossing. I was the only member of the military travelling on the ferry, so I tried to look serious and busy, as if I had been dispatched on an important and secret mission. The chafed leg was becoming increasingly burdensome after my rest, and my limping probably detracted from my appearance, though my ferry companions may have concluded that I had been injured at the front.

Having reached the opposite shore, I turned away from the big Englart highway and started towards Sunīši. It was a pleasant change to walk along the shady forest paths where, here and there on following a bend, a romantic villa would come into sight. The sound of a clarinet filled the space around a pink house with a big veranda and a balcony supported by white columns. The player was no virtuoso and the composition was not complicated – these were rather amateurish exercises, interrupted from time to time by wrong notes and determined efforts to start again from the beginning. Still these sounds in the shadowy coolness of the fir forest, not far from places where grenades were exploding in trenches, cannons rumbling, guns chattering and bayonets clinking, really moved me. I remembered evenings in our Riga apartment where a guest – and sometimes it was Tidriķis – sat down at the piano and, to the best of his or her ability, entertained us with the "Melancholy Waltz" or some other music… Perhaps it was no accident that I should remember Dārziņš and his "Melancholy Waltz" because it was in Murjāņi that he bought a house for his wife Anna and son Volfgangs.

The recorded and now remembered scenes contrast painfully with everything these places would have to endure, for soon none of the old farmsteads were left standing, and the municipal building, the school and the inn were all in ruins. Like some harbinger of doom I had walked just ahead of that destructive storm.

Lost in my reveries about music, I was startled by a cyclist riding towards me. As I'd discovered on various occasions that day, it's a small world, particularly when there's a war going on. I soon saw that the rider was K, the famous soloist of the Riga musical theatre and heart-throb of so many ladies. Although we were no more than casual acquaintances, having met only a couple of times at cultural events, we were so surprised to see each other that we started a conversation.

I asked if he was going to look for a safer place, but the famous singer bitterly pointed out that he had no home anywhere and therefore had no reason to move somewhere or look for shelter.

"I am a citizen of the world," he said mirthlessly. "I have no interest in politics. I have to sing where they pay me. It doesn't matter whether it's the Russians or the Germans, for we Latvians do not own anything, not even the ground on which we presently stand. All we can do is allow ourselves to be tossed about by others. Our history is not our own, but dictated by others. What can we desire, what can we hope for? Tell me if I'm wrong."

My train of thought differed little, I would say, from what K was saying, yet the way he said it, I found offensive, and it even made me angry. We said our goodbyes and I continued on my way in a depressed mood. I smoked several cigarettes, but even they did nothing to comfort me or give me pleasure. Only later did I understand that my body had detected the approaching fever – at the time I was convinced it was merely my reaction to what the soloist had said.

In the semi-darkness of the forest I had another encounter. Way ahead of me I spotted an old man who was walking slowly and using a wooden stick for support, so I soon caught up with him. I said hello but was not about to begin a long conversation. He was carrying a little sack over his shoulder, so I imagined that he had probably been visiting his relatives or neighbours.

"Are we travelling around our homeland?" he asked impishly.

"Yeah, I guess so," I replied.

For a while, we walked next to each other.

"Who'd have thought that at my age I too would have to hit the road," the old man said.

"So where are you going?" I asked without much interest.

"I'd be happy to know it myself," he said. "Nothing is known, nothing can be foreseen. Even now, for instance, we've no idea what's happening in Riga. And what will happen to us tomorrow? Though it seems that you've got it all figured out, haven't you, young man?"

He laughed but I did not reply.

"Go, go ahead at your own pace!" He stopped and waved his walking stick energetically. "Do not waste time because of me – my feet are old, and you'll simply tire of them."

Having walked out of the forest, I found a smoothly worked piece of wood and began to use it as a walking stick. It might well have served someone else for a similar purpose. It was a lucky coincidence, for almost half a kilometre later, two big dogs of an indeterminate breed ran out on to the road – maybe that's why this place bore the name of Suniši, Little Dogs – and I used my stick to teach them some respect. Probably the old man's stick will be of use to him for a similar purpose. For the most part, however, I did not lean on my stick but used it to kill time – rhythmically tapping sizeable roadside stones with it as I walked.

The sun was about to set, I could not have been too far from Englart and was getting quite tired. Judging by the map, I had covered about fifty kilometres in one day and that could have been too much. Of course, the broken boot and the chafed leg were an additional problem, but my general feeling was also adversely affected by a strange chill. I decided that it was time to look for a place to spend the night.

That night, barely dragging my feet, I walked past the place where several Latvian companies would soon have a nasty engagement with the Germans. Of the Latvians, who remained forever, I knew many quite well, including First Lieutenant Kaimiņš – he was heavily wounded in the head, however, miraculously survived his injury, got well and later served in a number of important posts in government institutions.

The scrubland on the edge of the forest a couple of kilometres from the Englart inn provided my shelter for the night. I deliberately chose a place that could not be noticed from either the road or any of the nearby houses. In the distance, past an uneven field, the barking of a dog could be heard, but I consoled myself with the thought that it could not have been my movement through the forest that set him off. Having found a more even spot, one without roots and fallen branches, I wrapped myself in my coat, sack under my head, and tried to fall asleep. Even though I was exhausted, I was wide awake. From the direction of Riga, cannon fire was heard that resembled the rumbling of distant thunder, but here in the forest, peace reigned in the company of nature's muffled sounds. As soon as I lay down, I began to shake with fever and sweat profusely, yet I didn't dare take off my overcoat. In my current situation, it wouldn't do to catch pneumonia or some other nasty illness. On that crisp August night, I could see stars amongst the branches overhead, and under the old leaves and mound of sand that served as my pillow I heard the rustling of tiny forest creatures.

I have no idea how long I lay in that state or at what moment I woke up and dozed off again. Several times it seemed to me that large or small animals were running by. Some of them even sounded human and, as I was groping for my revolver, I fell asleep again. Another approached me unseen with quick steps – probably a dog, fox or wolf – stopping at a safe distance and watching me carefully. As the wind blew into all the possible wooden instruments – pipes, clarinets, oboes, birch-bark trumpets and others, the entire forest, indeed the entire natural environment, came over to inspect this strange sleeper who had suddenly encroached upon their kingdom.

If I were buried or abandoned for dead in the open, these same beasts, bugs and tiny creatures would immediately attack me and tear at my flesh; they'd begin to eat me before I was cold. Soon enough, nothing much would remain of me – divided into bigger or smaller pieces I would be dispersed near and far, becoming part of these forests and fields, and what remained would gradually sink and turn into soil. I would become a handful of dust, a few elements of this land for which so much blood had been and would be shed. It could be said that those of us who were still alive and fighting, hating and killing one another, were battling with the remains of our ancestors: we trample them, ploughing and harrowing them; in the fall we harvest what has grown on them; we build our houses and temples on top of them; we feed on them. We cannot keep anything for ourselves. All that we think and do in our lives is either a revenge for or redemption of what our ancestors have experienced, or a hope for the future that our descendants will reap some benefit from our efforts. It is naive to hope for anything during our lifetime.

22 August

Soaking with sweat and deep into this kind of timeless reverie, I must have managed to fall asleep in the other half of the night, as I was woken by a cockerel crowing at a house nearby. Unlike our own one who lived with my parents, this one's song was somehow wrong, which amused me. And by that morning I needed some entertainment: during the night, as I tossed and turned, and a half-rotten birch branch was piercing my side, I'd put my head in a sandy hole and propped my legs on an incline. Upon waking my body ached as if someone had been hitting me with a stick all night. I stood up and almost fell down, since my legs did not want to obey me. Taking a few cautious steps whilst holding on to the trees, I managed to stretch them, then I quickly gathered my modest belongings and, through the bushes, made my way back to the road. The fever seemed to have abated.

Even though everything looked pale grey, the morning was clear and bright, the first rays were beginning to stream over the treetops and there wasn't a cloud in the sky. No drivers or pedestrians were to be seen and I began walking towards the River Brasla. Even though seemingly in working order, my legs hurt badly a few kilometres down the road, and I made a grave mistake in deciding to take a brief rest. I soon understood that after any – even the briefest – stop, it took quite a while to get going again at a halfway reasonable speed. So I decided to continue on my way without stopping unless there would be some special reason to do so. Because of my determination and willpower, I managed quite well for most of the day.

I had crossed the Brasla and covered half the distance to Lielstraupe before I realised that I'd forgotten my walking stick where I'd spent the night. The sun was already higher in the sky, the day was heating up and my stick would have come in handy not so much to chase away angry dogs as for additional support.

Some kilometres after Lielstraupe I came upon a field of rye and harvesters who had sat down to catch their breath and have lunch. There was an older man with a grey beard as well as three women: two young women who were probably sisters and perhaps the old man's daughters, and an older woman with a white headscarf, perhaps his wife and mother to his daughters, or maybe his sister.

Even though up to that moment I had been walking like some automaton, I did not want to be impolite and, after exchanging greetings, stopped and was even happy to accept their invitation to join them.

"Rye has to be harvested and potatoes dug. How could we run at this time?" the old man replied calmly when I asked if they might be thinking of leaving. He already knew about the German attack on Riga.

"And the cattle, what can we do with the cattle?" the woman added.

The young ones didn't say anything, just kept eyeing me secretly (or so they thought), whispering and giggling.

I was offered a piece of rye bread, cottage cheese and a cool, fermented drink from a jug, and I felt as if I'd never had a more delicious meal. No matter how crazy their talk was, it lifted my heart and filled it with peace. These feelings were entirely different from those provoked by my meeting with the soloist K.

Upon finishing my meal I thanked the harvesters, said goodbye and continued on my way. At first it was torture, as my muscles were stiff from my having stopped and sat down. The last thing I wanted was to reveal this to the two young ladies, so with teeth clenched I marched bravely to the first bend in the road, and only when I was convinced that no one could see me did I allow myself to slow down and even limp slightly.

I could not hope to cover much distance that day and was relieved when, in the afternoon, I spotted the bright surface of Lake Ungurs and the turret of the Unguri chapel behind a hillock, where I intended to look for a place to rest and spend the night.

This time I had very good luck in my search for shelter. In a house on the lakeshore I met a lone old woman. All the rest of her people had gone away, leaving the property in her care.

"I have to die soon anyway," she said and let me use the granary for the night. Since it was still quite early and I did not feel like sleeping, I sat on the jetty over the lake, soaking my feet and noting the events of the past couple of days.

23 August

I slept badly. Again I had a fever, sweated a lot and fell asleep only towards the morning when it seemed to be getting close to dawn. Soon I woke up, put on my boots and clothes, and set off on my way. It was a remarkably quiet and foggy morning. A peaceful wartime morning. It was impossible to see very far ahead, and the milky white air seemed to echo the slightest sound: water dripping from the branches of the trees lining the sides of the road; the flapping of wings; the thud with which an apple fell to the ground; the bellowing of stags in the forest's depths. The fever had abated and, even though I was groggy and stiff, I found it pleasurable to breathe in the cool air, and felt some joy in my heart. I was determined to get to Valmiera the same day and was sure that I could do it. I was a little less sure of what awaited me there.

For quite some time, I met neither pedestrians nor drivers, and noticed some bustle only as I approached Ungurmuiža. I stepped off the road and, using the utmost caution, tried to steal past the manor house. The fog served me well: it gave me such good cover that no one could see me. It was clear that some army unit was stationed at the manor – horses were braying and there was shouting and cursing in Russian. Keeping within the shadows of the large oak trees in the park, I'd crept quite close and could now observe what was happening in front of the manor. There were several carts, and smoke was billowing from a bonfire around which a number of posh chairs and even a sofa, apparently brought out from the manor house, were placed. Under the open windows of the house, various pieces of broken furniture, picture frames and other objects lay scattered about. Most of the windows had been broken and the building had the look of a blind man who'd lost his way in the confusing surroundings.

Watching the behaviour and general mood of the soldiers I concluded that this had to be a "revolutionary" unit that had gone over to the Bolsheviks and for that very reason I should be on my way as quickly and inconspicuously as possible. I didn't feel at all sorry for the devastation wrought on the manor – it was just what the supporters of one foreign power had done to what belonged to another foreign power. It was just one of many manors: an embodiment and symbol of the wrongs visited upon my people over a period of seven hundred years. It was the cornerstone and buttress of foreign powers.

And then I almost got myself into a fix by attracting attention: when, having reached what seemed to be a safe distance from the manor, I returned to the road, three big dogs of some exquisite breed emerged from the fog and drew close to me, running across the field. They did not bark and that made me all the more anxious, for everyone knows that a barking dog is less dangerous than one that advances on you silently. I'd already drawn my revolver, but had the presence of mind not to shoot – having sniffed me the dogs lost all interest and soon ran off on other canine business.

Had I not kept a cool head and pulled the trigger, the noise would have certainly alarmed the army unit housed at the manor and, who knows, that day could have been my last. I must note, however, that the feeling of fear that clouds the mind was quite alien to me. I cannot claim to be completely without fear, but I've noticed since my early youth that at moments when others, overtaken by fear, take flight, lose their bearings and probably get into even worse trouble, I am overcome by an unusual peace and serenity, with my mind working as precisely as clockwork. It may of course be some special kind of insensitivity. I have been reproached at times for being too direct and sharp-tongued in social settings, even where it concerns the ladies, because I tend to speak my mind. It is my belief that if it is the truth, one should not fear it. And there should be no fear in hearing it. Perhaps it is cruel at times but some white lies, told out of pity, to me are simply a sign of cowardice.

Fear and cowardice are feelings unworthy of a man – they are something from the animal world, something rudimentary, as unnecessary and unseemly as body hair. Some miles past Ungurmuiža, I spied some live creature on the road. At first, it was just a small, moving point but, on getting closer, I realised that it was a fox. In another instant, I could see that it was not going in the same direction as I but coming towards me. Most fascinating was the fact that the stupid fox didn't notice me for quite a while and only at a very short distance it suddenly froze, pricked its ears and stared straight at me fearfully. I too stopped, for now, after what I had seen at the manor and the experience with the dogs, I found this meeting amusing. The very next instant, the fox demonstrated the ridiculous essence of its animal nature – it swung around at lightning speed and fled, moreover running not to the bushes lining the ditch or into the forest, but straight down the road, disappearing behind the bend. Fear is an animal instinct. This is proven also by the fact that no forest animal, from a poisonous snake to a wolf or a bear, will attack a person just like that. An animal is afraid of man, for over millennia it has been proven time and again that man is superior. That is if he's not of the faint-hearted.

At that moment I had no inkling that the day's adventures were not yet over. Now my route took me past another place important to the sad history of our people. The Rubene Church was said to be the place where the man known as Henricus Lettus, or Henry of Livonia, the author of the famous chronicle, worked and baptised the first Livs.

34

It was in fact the very first Christian church, spreading that alien faith throughout our land. By Kokkenhof I was forced to come back on to the big road and there I immediately got into trouble.

I noticed the three riders only after they had seen me. It would have been silly to run or show any resistance, for that would have certainly ended very badly for me. "Stoi!" they yelled at me, then rode up to me and demanded to see my documents. Since I'd had no chance to obtain any kind of travel documents in Riga, I tried to convince them that I was on my way back to my unit, but they did not believe this story. I heard them suggest that I was probably either a deserter who had gone over to the Bolsheviks or perhaps even a German spy. I was lucky that it did not occur to them to finish me off right there and then. Having taken away my revolver, they made me follow them.

I hadn't expected that my journey could end like this and was sure that sooner or later I would find a way to escape. My situation was not good, but neither was it hopeless. The riders now had to adjust to my walking speed; I was walking in the middle of the road, two of them were flanking me on each side, and the third one was keeping an eye on me and from time to time nudged me from the back. In this formation, we entered the manor grounds. Several artillerymen were busy by the horse barns, one of the buildings – it may have been the factor's home – served as a headquarters and a messenger emerged from it and quickly mounted his horse. I felt that everyone we encountered looked at us and tried to guess who the devil had been caught this time.

I was brought inside and turned over to two soldiers who proceeded to lock me up in a dank and empty cellar. The space had a clay floor and, by the very ceiling, a tiny window, the size of a fist. Naturally enough, there was no furniture and no conveniences of any kind. I spread out my great coat and lay down on it. There was no hope to break out of these thick walls, my sore feet needed a rest and – who knows? – after a nap an escape plan just might come to mind.

And yet there was no time to rack my brain over any escape plans. I must have fallen fast asleep, for I was startled by a rough kick to my side and a guard's voice: "Vstavai!" I had no sense of how long I'd slept, but the light on the upper floor suggested that it was probably late in the afternoon. I was brought into a room that in peacetime must have served as a dining room, for there was still a sideboard with china by the wall and the large table was requisitioned for the war effort. A gaunt non-commissioned officer in the dragoons was sitting at the table. "Gaunt" may not even begin to describe it: he was one of those people whose bodies in childhood and throughout their lives seem not only too tall but also too thin in every aspect. Even his face was thin, and his uniform looked like there was no flesh inside at all. He had a sickly grey face, a sparse moustache and equally sparse, slicked-back yellowish hair. The ceaseless smoking did not make him look any healthier: he was smoking as I walked in, kept lighting cigarettes during our conversation and remained smoking when I left his "office".

"Ivan Petrovich Herzenfeld," he introduced himself. In his civilian life, he must be a quiet, timid, even shy person, always dissatisfied with himself and full of various prejudices. Yet the circumstances of army and war had brought him to this situation, and he had learnt to hide his congenital shortcomings behind theatrical gestures and rituals. Smoking undoubtedly was one of them. During our conversation, he casually offered me a cigarette, but I politely declined. Amongst his means of expressing himself was also "manly" yelling. It was clear that by this he was trying to win greater respect, yet the impression it made was more comical than anything else.

Whatever the form this meeting took, its content was far from comical. He inquired as to my political views, my attitude towards the provisional government and the

Bolsheviks. I answered truthfully, indicating both that I consider the provisional government to be weak and that I feel no sympathy towards the Bolsheviks. "Is that so?" That was the extent of my interrogator's response. Having asked another couple of questions which were clearly clumsily laid traps, he announced that he would have me court-martialled. That was not good at all, for in all likelihood it meant being executed. I threw a glance at the open window, but the officer had immediately caught my movement and said in a stage voice: "If you attempt to run, we'll shoot you ourselves."

I had to return to my cell, yet here fortune suddenly smiled upon me. As the guard and I were descending, it was good old Tidriķis we encountered coming up the stairs. He was taken completely aback by seeing me. He almost passed me by without paying the slightest attention but then – honour where honour is due – he quickly grasped the seriousness of the situation and acted accordingly.

"Where are you taking him?" he sternly demanded.

"To the cellar, Your Excellency!"

"Bring him to me," Tidriķis waved casually.

"Yes sir, Your Excellency!"

And so I came to be in the company of my good friend. It turned out that the manor housed not only dragoon units and artillerymen, but also what remained of Tidriķis's regiment after the battles near Riga and the retreat in the course of two days. True to form, he had settled in probably the cosiest space of the factor's house, the veranda, within hours making it conform to his tastes and lifestyle. Had our meeting not taken place under wartime conditions and had I not been facing court martial moments before, one would have thought that we were two people enjoying a country retreat.

"We just got here today and – what do you know? – you're already here!" Tidriķis seemed amused as he offered me some sweet wine and cigarettes. We sat in wicker garden chairs, the slanting rays of the August sun were coming in through the small panes of the veranda windows, and the air quavered from the smoke of our cigarettes and flickered with shiny motes. Next to maps and dirty dishes, I saw several of Tidriķis's books – Thucydides's *History of the Peloponnesian War* in Latin and Clausewitz's *On War*. I knew that the object of Tidriķis's interest was not the history or theory of the art of war or individual battles, but the past as such. Depending on political events and even his own matters of the heart or family circumstances, he used to find in testimonies from the past what seemed to him most relevant, and thus tried to find a deeper explanation for what was happening in the present.

He never parted with history books, although I have no idea when he managed to read them. "I don't read, I study," he once explained. My occasional experience suggested that studying meant lengthy periods of reflection, staring at the same page until the student dozed off and woke up with a start only when the pencil he had been hitherto holding in his hand fell to the floor and rolled off.

I did not refuse the drink he offered me and told him about my troubles.

"Goddamn Herzenfeld," Tidriķis grumbled. "He is neither a real Russian, nor a German, so he just stirs up shit wherever he can."

In the cosy atmosphere of Tidriķis's "office" we worked out my escape plan. Ignoring my protestations, Tidriķis first of all got me a fine lunch: he asked for some boiled potatoes, bread, cottage cheese and sour cream, and "if possible, also a piece of meat". No piece of meat was immediately available, but that fact notwithstanding, it was one of the best meals I've ever had.

"Victory is usually based not on physical but moral superiority," Tidriķis said. "By the way, that's why this war is a completely hopeless undertaking. Physical superiority is like lottery winnings – sometimes one side gets it, at other times the other does, but, if there is no moral superiority on either side, it is clear that this war will have no winners. The only possible winners may be the Bolsheviks with their fervent speeches and sheer pluck."

At the basis of our plan was this very theory, probably borrowed from Clausewitz, as well as our belief that, to a great degree, luck depends on the ability to surprise the enemy when he least expects it. "There is no way of knowing what Herzenfeld might think of next, so let's not waste time," Tidriķis said. Since my revolver had been taken away, Tidriķis produced a Smith & Wesson from his stores, but we agreed that I should put it to use only in extraordinary, not to say completely hopeless, circumstances. A gift even more valuable than the S & W was several travel documents stamped with the headquarters' emblem with blank spots in which I could enter any destination I chose.

Wine, cigarettes, lunch and conversation became a kind of overture or introduction to our plan, for afterwards we entered the house from the veranda as two war buddies deep in an important discussion. I've already mentioned my lack of fear and here this character trait served me particularly well. The main thing that was to attract attention was the naturalness of our performance and the objective Tidriķis had set for us: to get past the sentries posted outside the factor's house and at the gate to the property. Apparently our performance was impeccable, for neither in the yard nor on the road did anyone pay attention to us. At the root of our success was of course the fact that during the time of our meeting and conversation, the guards had changed and both those who captured me and those who imprisoned me were off-duty.

I said goodbye to Tidriķis, thanking him sincerely and, without much worry, started out in the direction of Valmiera. I was sure that no one would come after me, and the main thing was to take care to never run into Herzenfeld again.

I never saw Tidriķis after that. Several years later, I found out that in the winter of 1919 he was captured by the Bolsheviks, who beat and tortured him as a vicious reprisal and eventually abandoned him tied to a tree in the forest where he froze to death.

I stumbled into Valmiera in the late afternoon. For the first time in days, I no longer had to hide so much, yet I remained cautious. Surprisingly, I found shelter at an inn where I could wash and generally clean up. I settled into a room that for a few days would serve as my improvised headquarters. Having slightly changed my outer appearance, I took care of a few important matters whilst also trying to find out about the situation in the city and perhaps hear some news from the front. I concluded that infantry alone would not be enough to take Valmiera.

My first task of course was to take care of my boots. Since I didn't have an extra pair, I had to wait for the cobbler to finish the job. I questioned him about the mood in the city and soon found out that this simple man had also fallen victim to Bolshevik proselytisers. Clearly his services are used by people of different classes and levels of prosperity, so some diligent agitator must have had boots or shoes to mend. He must have filled the poor man's head with the benefits to the nation and the cobbler of a government of workers and peasants, one without masters and servants and no classes whatsoever.

There was something unnerving and perhaps religious in the conviction with which the old man explained the great plans for changing the world. He truly believed in what he'd been told and promised, and I remembered with annoyance what Tidriķis had said about moral superiority.

"Your time has passed," the cobbler said, handing me the boots. They, however, were in perfect order now and the old hypocrite did not refuse my money, which I found somewhat amusing. In some sense, this was a just redistribution of wealth. Now I could walk incomparably better, so I quickly made my way to visit Madame B.

Here I have to digress to say a few words about her. Madame B is my distant relative, my mother's aunt. A widow for the past ten years or even a little longer. Her husband was an artillery officer who, in 1906 at Port Arthur, was wounded in both legs, shell-shocked and taken prisoner by the Japanese. After being liberated, he was given the Order of St George, but of course did not return to active duty. Four years later, he passed away. According to conventional wisdom, his health, ruined in war and captivity, was at fault, but I remember my parents sometimes mentioned, half-jokingly, that Madame B had somehow managed to get rid of her limping and slightly eccentric husband herself. As far as I know, no concrete accusations or evidence ever saw the light of day, yet the suspicion itself lent additional colour to the already odious image of Madame.

Madame E used hints, behaviour and her outer appearance to create her desired image of a mysterious person with paranormal powers. Even her makeup – particularly the way she painted her eyebrows – seemed to emphasise that she saw, knew and understood much more than the rest of us, and that she might have a close relationship with other worlds and supernatural beings. My father used to laughingly call Madame B the old witch, but it was easy to see that, even though he was much younger than Madame, he too had a hard time resisting the power of her magic. Ever since Madame B became a widow, she was always accompanied by spiritually inclined youths who avidly soaked up her theories and experiences in foreign lands. In just a couple of years, she visited myriad countries: she rode a camel by the pyramids of Egypt, toured Palestine and visited Constantinople; in 1911, she made a special trip to Paris to see the "empty space" replacing the stolen portrait of Mona Lisa and a year before the war, she almost married an Indian rajah. Madame was in the habit of conducting spiritualist seances; every six months she claimed to have discovered a new and particularly useful method for eating, breathing or taking physical exercise; she often came up with dances of her own choreography; in her spare moments she painted naive little pictures; and she complained to anyone who would listen that in her youth she'd missed an opportunity to have a brilliant career in the moving pictures (at other times she mentioned the operetta or music hall) in Berlin.

Now I stood outside the house of B. It was a two-storey building with a lavish, albeit not particularly well-tended, garden. Madame's chambermaid opened the door and announced that the lady of the house was away. In accordance with Madame B's taste, the maid was wearing a long Oriental robe and her dark hair was gathered with a fancy ribbon – I thought she looked like a gypsy. I left a note mentioning my visit and left.

With at least a few hours to spare, I killed time by walking down to the Gauja by the old castle ruin. The Gauja has always seemed to me the most interesting of our rivers. Albeit not as wide as the Daugava or the Lielupe, it is substantially longer, curvier and more varied. Rapids, streams, whirlpools, undertows, rocky banks, caves and quicksand, deadly for an unsuspecting swimmer – all of this made the Gauja a challenging opponent, not unlike those I've encountered in chess and sport: always pleasant to come up against. I threw off all my clothing on a white sandbank and jumped into the murky, fast-flowing water. Since early childhood on the shores of Lake Ķīšezers, I'd been an agile swimmer, and soon reached the opposite bank and dived to the darkest depths without too much effort. Moving my arms and legs vigorously, I then swam against the current for a while, only to let it float me back downstream as I caught my breath. I came out of the water refreshed and in a good mood. In fact I cannot remember ever being in such an uncharacteristically optimistic state of mind. I dropped to the ground and let the sun dry me off, then I put on my clothes and went back to Madame's.

Presently, the maid let me in without a word and asked me to wait a moment. That moment went on for some time, and I took the opportunity to examine the eclectic decor: shelves with woodcarvings of scary African idols; a statue of Buddha sitting on a small sideboard in the corner; a zigzag-patterned woven rug which my mind transformed into the topographical map of a fantastical region. I wondered if the scent that lingered in the air was some peculiar kind of tobacco, myrrh or perhaps some other aromatic substance brought from faraway lands.

And then she arrived, as always making a theatrical entrance. The door to the second floor had opened soundlessly and I heard her voice from the top of the stairs: "Hail, my stately warrior!"

There she stood, dressed in a long, black cape embroidered with golden ornaments and adorned with many heavy gold pieces of jewellery. Her entrance must have been well thought-out, and probably rehearsed many times before and repeated often. Everything was of importance: her location at the top of the stairs, the evening light, streaming that precise moment through one of the second-floor windows and making her gold glow. Her thick, dark hair was gathered in a large knot held together by a golden, bejewelled clasp. Since the death of her husband and her subsequent long journeys, her face – even in the darkest months of winter – was browned by the sun and her tan was rendered even more striking by her bright lipstick and eyeshadow. I must admit that I had no difficulty understanding the force of Madame's attraction, which she deployed to overpower not only the submissive seekers of spirituality but even those who moved in spiritualist circles, or tough characters like my father. She extended her bejewelled hand and it was a sign that I should ascend and kiss it.

The scent of bittersweet spices wafted over me and, accompanied by the sound of invisible tinkling beads, we entered Madame B's salon. Madame sat down on a sofa and, with a gesture, invited me to take a seat next to her. I declined politely and sat down on a chair. She lit a cigarette in a long holder, looked me up and down with heavy-lidded eyes and asked where I was coming from and where I was going. I briefly told her of my plans, supplementing them with my very recent idea of finding my way to Finland and then to some other foreign land.

Madame B seemed, however, hardly interested in my comings and goings: to her, I was simply an unexpected guest sent her way by providence – one who would be ready, or rather obliged, to listen to her latest "theories". I already knew that Madame B fancied herself a follower of Helena Blavatsky and a local expert on theosophy, yet I had never encountered this "science" of hers directly. Here I must note that I have always been a rational person, with no interest or belief whatsoever in supernatural phenomena, ghosts, otherworldly life, astrology or spiritualism. Equally, I have no time for religion or gods as, to be frank, I've never felt the need that would justify such constructs of human consciousness. Thus it's easily understood that for me Madame B's "lecture", albeit amusing, was quite an ordeal.

"What we're experiencing right now," Madame B said, slowly stretching her vowels, "is the beginning of the Age of Aquarius. It's been common knowledge since ancient times that the position of the stars and astrological eras have a direct impact on mankind. The destruction of the world at the time of Noah, the slavery of the Jews in Egypt, their return to the Promised Land, wars, famine and disaster, the rise and fall of the Roman Empire – all of this has been determined not so much by divine providence, but by the movement, gravitation and placement of heavenly bodies.

44

Which, of course, does not exclude the possibility that God or gods control them. Or maybe peoples of yore considered the planets and stars to be gods. It is written in ancient manuscripts that the Age of Aquarius will be marked by increased yearning for freedom and idealism on the one hand, and unprecedented ruthlessness, bloodshed and violence on the other. Never before has there existed an opportunity to kill so many people as there is now. And never before has this opportunity been grasped with such alacrity. The Great War has brought it all upon us; the world as we knew it is crumbling and no one knows what will arise from its smouldering ruins. Rulers fall or are chased from their thrones, states dissolve and all kinds of opportunists in search of power, who never had a say, are champing at the bit..."

I listened to Madame B wearily and mused that the secret to the attraction of that science of hers was the skilful way she wrapped events, facts and commonplace truths in an esoteric veil and presented them as supernatural revelations. It was no more than the skill found in marketplace fortune tellers who extract all kinds of prophecies out of you and then to your great surprise restate them to you at an exorbitant cost.

"And what will happen now?" I asked without much enthusiasm.

"The anointed will survive and they will take power!" Madame B opened her eyes wide; she looked like a madwoman. "And all the rest will serve them, albeit unawares. Various false teachings and ideologies will sink into oblivion, but the power of the anointed and the reciprocal bonds between them shall remain obscure to everyone else..."

Much to my relief, the maid appeared in the doorway at this very moment and asked us to lunch.

The small dining area in the adjoining room was furnished in a similar manner to what I'd seen of the rest of the house. Exotic curiosities from faraway lands were on the walls, the bright late-afternoon sun was shining through the wide, open window, and canaries were busying around in a sizeable cage.

The meal, which consisted of rice and spices, and had a curious aroma, was put on the table; wine was poured into goblets.

I was about to taste the food, but with the slightest of gestures Madame B prevented me from doing so. She put her hands on the table, closed her eyes and quietly murmured some incantation or prayer. I think I heard her mention Isis, but I may have been mistaken.

Immediately afterwards with an encouraging gesture, she invited me to partake of the meal.

"A strong, young man like yourself might wonder why I feed you a meal without meat," she said. "I have been observing vegetarianism for many years, and believe me – a meatless meal provides a person with all that is needed, and the power concealed in it is even greater than in animal products. No creature need be killed for a person to be well fed. This simple truth is particularly important to remember as we face this terrible war."

After the meal, we returned to the salon where tea and nut cookies were served.

"Where were we..." Madame B thought a moment. "Oh yes, I was telling you about the Age of Aquarius. We must keep in mind that this time can bring great achievements and unseen discoveries to mankind, but it may equally be the case that the knowledge and new discoveries end up with the forces of darkness, and power is usurped by a faction of renegades who do not believe in anything or anyone, and the Age of Darkness ensues!"

An awkward silence set in. She no longer spoke, and I didn't really have anything to say. The birds were chirping pleasantly in their cage, but in the distance some shots rang out.

"Yes, but..." I tried to maintain the conversation, "is there anything we can do to change this?"

Madame B seemed to have expected precisely this kind of question. Her eyes glittering, she leaned forward and whispered: "Of course, young man! Only – are you ready for it?"

"Ready? For what?" I was confused.

"According to the Great Wisdom, all that happens in the macrocosm is reflected in every person, or the microcosm, and yet what happens in a person can be reflected in the macrocosm, but only if that person possesses Knowledge!"

Madame B stretched out a cigarette case that was encrusted with filigree ivory ornaments and I took a cigarette without thinking. She smoked thin cigarettes that smelt of cloves, cinnamon and some other overseas spices, but my own cigarette was different. The smoke did not taste at all of tobacco – it must have been some mixture of Madame's "magic" herbs. Not being easily frightened, and convinced that my mother's aunt would hardly try to poison me – she would only serve me up some opium or another exotic intoxicant – I nonchalantly smoked as if such cigarettes had been my routine since adolescence.

"You say that we have never controlled anything in the history of our people, that everything has always been decided by alien masters and alien powers..." she said.

I could not recall saying anything of the kind to her, but I had thought it often.

"You think that the Great Wisdom about which I began to tell you is just another ruse of alien masters..."

I had no answer to this, yet I knew for sure that I did not say this to her either, though I'd considered doing so.

"But that's not the case!" She stood up abruptly. "The Great Wisdom has not been invented or composed by some person. The Great Wisdom has been passed down to us. The Great Wisdom can give everyone the strength to change their own destinies as well as those of whole cities, peoples, nations and countries. The Great Wisdom is the truth!"

Had I not partaken of Madame B's weird cigarettes, I probably would have laughed out loud or uttered some sceptical wisecrack, but now my head was full of emptiness that resembled the white morning mist and I could not produce a sound.

"It is a good thing that you do not believe in anything, do not trust anyone and are afraid of nothing." Madame B kept staring into my eyes. "Hope is the consolation of fools, you say…"

"Did I say that?" It flashed through my foggy brain.

"Nothing is sacred to you; you are like an empty vessel that cannot be filled with anything because it has been tightly shut with all kinds of seals. Come!"

She stretched out a white hand with red-painted fingernails, her golden bangles jangling and her rings flashing. I got up and followed her like a sleepwalker or someone hypnotised and in a trance. Moreover, one part of my consciousness – the part that at other times would have been given to doubting, resisting and objecting – was still full of the fog caused by the inhaled substances and remained seated in the deep armchair, whereas some other corner of my awareness had retained an admirable acuity of perception and thought, and let me get up and follow Madame B. The senses of this other me seized on the most minute nuance of sound that wafted in through the open window, the tiniest suggestion of a scent or dust mite, and each step I made on the ornamented rugs may have been a small achievement to some people, but to me it seemed a truly magnificent and significant achievement for all mankind.

25 August

I woke up in bright daylight in a large bed with white, starched sheets. My clothes, cleaned and ironed, were next to the bed on a chair, my boots were polished to a shine and even my rucksack knapsack on the floor looked new – carefully organised, and closed with an elegant knot. On the wall I spotted a painting: pastel hues depicting a romantic garden where, shaded by trees, fairies, elves, satyrs and other fairy-tale characters were lounging about. Many of these were either half or completely naked, but didn't appear to be in the least embarrassed by their nakedness while they refreshed themselves in a small lake or played some mysterious games in a sunny glade.

On the other side of the bed there was a jug, a bowl and a white towel, and on the wall there was a small mirror in a bronze frame. The window was open, so I could hear clatter of hooves, rumbling of carts and soldiers calling to each other.

Since my arrival at Madame B's, two nights and a day had passed, yet at that moment, I was not aware of it. My head was perfectly clear, my body, strong and rested, and I had no suspicion that some things might have been lost from my consciousness because of intoxicating substances.

I sat up and at that very moment remembered what I thought to be the previous evening: Madame B's strange cigarettes, our conversation and the moment when she asked me to come with her. I'd got up and gone... Yes, but where did I go?

Sitting on the edge of the bed, I gradually remembered the scenes that could only have been a strikingly realistic dream. It's nonsensical to call a dream realistic – I should probably use the word phantasmagorical.

I did not consider it more than a dream, however. The appearance of dreams in our consciousness is nothing supernatural. Just by paying a little attention to their content, it soon becomes clear that a dream is not something we've experienced throughout the night but rather a phenomenon that appears in our consciousness either at the very moment of waking or even a moment afterwards, as – now being awake – we're trying to remember things of which we can have no memories.

A strange and immaculate space emerged in front of my eyes. Some voices were heard although I seemed to be alone in the room. I had a bright yellow bracelet of some unfamiliar material around my wrist and instinctively – as if obeying some inaudible orders – I understood that I must get completely naked. Then my senses led me to a large wash-room where, according to one's wishes, warm or cold water streamed from the ceiling and the air was full of aromatic steam, birdsong and joyful splashing. Having washed and wrapped myself in a white, fluffy towel, I went upstairs and wound up in a large, brightly lit room. All around me there were pools of various sizes – big and quadrangular, irregular, and even very small and round. In each, the water looked different – in one it swelled and rippled like the sea, in another it boiled like some hellish cauldron, and in yet another, tiny bubbles floated endlessly to the surface. Somehow I understood that I had to get into these pools, but the only way to do it was to climb up to the very ceiling and then slide down through wide, meandering pipes. I could continue on my way only after I had soaked in every one of the pools and slid down each of the garishly coloured pipes.

The next challenge was considerably more difficult. I found myself confronted with several doors. One of them was undoubtedly the exit, but to locate it I had to enter all the others. Behind each one, some torture awaited me. Thus, for instance, the first one was full of thick, hot steam that was fragrant with exotic herbs. I could only last a few moments there and rushed out and through the next door. Behind it was something resembling a country bathhouse with its benches to sweat it out, but there too the heat was so savage and dry that I could only stay for a minute. Luckily, behind another door, there were small chambers where icy cold or boiling hot water was pouring down from the walls and ceiling. At times it came down with a big splash, at others it turned into tiny, prickly needles, and a couple of jets of cold water left me nicely refreshed.

Only two doors remained, and, with some trepidation, I opened the first. It was neither warm nor cold there, and the shady room resembled a mountain cave. Jagged mineral icicles dangled from the ceiling, but at the far end of the cave I noticed a stone slab and knew that I had to lie down there. As soon as I did, something extraordinary happened: a barely audible music seemed to start up – tinkling or the splashing of waves. Before my eyes, constellations lit up and I could no longer sense my body. It seemed as though my flesh no longer belonged to me or that I had left it lying on the stone, whereas I had become pure spirit. I was absolutely free, not in some concrete sense but in all possible senses – so free that I was capable of anything: both noble and lofty plans and actions, and the basest and meanest acts and cruelties. I felt the way a newborn might feel if only self-awareness were available to a newborn's senses and mind; I felt like a newborn in front of whom all life lies wide open and anything is possible: to become a genius or the ruler of some country, or end life in poverty or on the gallows. It's not hope that's important, I suddenly realised, but opportunity. Babies have no hope – hope is what their parents have. And only when one fails to find and fulfil an opportunity, only then hope turns out to be the consolation of fools.

I must have dozed off, if that's possible in a dream, for I started up with a sensation of falling: I had returned to my body and was lying in the mysterious cave on a stone slab. The music had stopped, stars faded, it was almost completely dark in the room and, sliding my palm along the rough wall, I was feeling my way to the exit. In the anteroom, I was dazzled by white brightness that felt like the intensity of lightning, and I unconsciously touched my lips and tasted the bitterness of salt. The brightness had come from a small black box that was placed in the middle of the room. I walked around it cautiously and on the other side of the box noticed some kind of window from which light emanated, and in that window, there I was – the way I had come out of the dark cave a minute ago, dressed in a white nightgown, hand clasped over my mouth – but I was very,

very small. It could have even been a photographic image if it weren't colourful, as in real life, and if it hadn't produced light. On the box, in tiny letters, it said "Lumix" – an indecipherable and probably magic derivation of the Latin word for light. I opened the last door and here I was – sitting on the edge of the bed in Madame B's white room. I picked up a glass from the nightstand and noticed that it was almost empty – either I'd drunk it in my semi-awake state or it had evaporated at an incredible speed; and then, a split second later, I almost dropped the glass…

"Excuse me, I didn't know you were awake. I was coming to wake you up." I had missed the opening of the door, but there she was – the maid was standing on the threshold. "Breakfast is served."

After getting up, washing and shaving, I savoured the moment of dressing in my cleaned and ironed clothes, and went to the dining room. The table had been set for me alone. There was a pot with fragrant coffee, three boiled eggs, a healthy portion of bread and even ham.

"Is the lady of the house not having breakfast?" I asked the maid.

"Oh, not at all! The lady set out already last night," the maid answered. "But you should have a really good breakfast! I know that you are not a vegetarian, so I got you some ham and eggs."

I put three teaspoons of sugar in my coffee, added some milk and considered what I had just heard. Only now it dawned on me that I must have slept for not just one night but also the following day and another night. I decided not to ask about Madame B's esoteric travels, for it was none of my business. If the maid proved to have a loose tongue and decided to tell me herself, so be it.

After such a long sleep, I felt quite hungry indeed, so I quickly polished off everything on the table (for a minute or two I did feel embarrassed about my gluttony), drank as much as three cups of coffee and was ready to be on my way.

"Madame asked me to give you this." The maid handed me a grey envelope by the door. I said goodbye and went out on the street. It was still very early: the first sunrays were barely reaching above the tops of the trees, the grass was covered in white dew and the air retained the night chill. I stopped by the gate and tore open the envelope. Inside I found a grainy sheet of letter paper with a watermark, which smelt of clove oil. "Dr Mežulis at the Institution for Curing and Assisting the Unsound of Mind in Strenči," it read. And also: "I see people, they look like trees walking around. And trees walking like people." The penultimate sentence I recognised as a quote from the Gospel of Mark and, to be exact, from the story of Jesus curing a blind man, but the last sentence remained obscure to me. I decided that perhaps Madame B wanted to let me know where she had gone, and so I began to walk in the direction of Strenči myself.

It was a beautiful morning, in fact the most beautiful of all mornings in the past few days, for inexplicably my heart was full of peace and my consciousness of the certainty that I would reach a definite goal and all my life would possess a meaning I had hitherto been unaware of. Previously such feelings and thoughts would have been entirely alien to me, but now I accepted them as natural and self-explanatory. My flesh was now rested and strong, and without the slightest exertion and doubt I went towards the fulfilment of my destiny. And only now and then, for instance, during a brief rest on a stone bridge over a pleasant gurgling brook, was I plagued by something like a doubt: am I really moving and acting of my own free will? And if I'm following the directions of my own mind, why is it that, besides this empty physical strength and sense of purpose, I'm not aware of anything else? As in a fairy tale, someone had ordered me – cast a spell over me – to travel to no one knows where and bring no one knows what, without explaining the details. Am I still under the influence of the strange dream? Or is it Madame B's esoteric sorcery?

To distract myself from those thoughts I began contemplating my steps, yielding to their brisk and uniform rhythm, and decided to ignore the poles marking the distance in versts. I'd already noticed that as soon as you begin to walk "from post to post", time seems to stand still and you don't seem to be making any progress. You're soon overcome by exhaustion and impotence, and begin moving ever slower, while your physical strength drains away and your determination and energy wane.

Leaving that aside, the walk was rather monotonous, for the forest stretched almost uninterrupted along the road: only a couple of times did I notice some houses in the distance and hear the barking of dogs. Luckily the dogs showed no sign of wanting to attack or follow me. Every once in a while I heard the angry hiss of locomotives behind the forest on the right – both my former comrades in arms and ordinary people longing for security were moving rapidly on the rails towards the east. Yet I didn't envy them, nor did I envy cart drivers who caught up with me from time to time and offered me a ride. I thanked them but declined politely, hinting that I had some special task that I would not to reveal to anyone.

Strangely enough, I too had begun to believe in this story, even though I had no idea what it was that I should accomplish.

I was tormented by such fruitless musings until the very moment when I came upon the railroad crossing and realised that I had reached Strenči. I'd never been in this area before, but it soon became clear to me that it was impossible to get lost here. Strenči was a very small village with only one road cutting through it, and there, on the side of this road and under some leafy trees, was the recently built Institution for Curing and Assisting the Unsound of Mind.

After entering the gate and seeing an imposing tower right in front of me, I became a little nervous – I felt that a host of mentally unbalanced individuals were ready to pounce on me. Here and there amongst the park trees, I spied buildings resembling holiday homes, but didn't meet any lunatics. Two older ladies were strolling towards me, so I turned to them as I wanted to know where I could find Dr Mežulis. The ladies were very responsive and offered to walk me to what they called the New House.

"It is right here, go straight and then to the right," one of them suggested, following me.

"Yes, thank you so much," I said, but the lady would not leave.

"It is right here, right here," she repeated.

"Thank you, I am really grateful to you," I replied.

"Are you here to stay?" she finally asked.

"No, no, I am just going to visit Dr Mežulis," I said quickly and slipped into the building to which I had been steered.

Dr Mežulis surprised me with his dazzling whiteness: it seemed he was emanating light. The doctor was a short man with completely white hair and an equally white, well-tended beard. And his coat was also impeccably white.

"Good day, good day, young Mr X," he was walking towards me with arms spread wide, like a long-missed relative or family friend. This may be the place to point out that my actual name or last name is of no import in these notes; it can change or be changed at will, yet such changes would neither add something to the narrative nor take it away. I could be simply Someone or, even better, Something, for there were way too many like me in these chaotic times and – I am sure of it – there will be in generations to come.

"My pleasure." That was all that I managed to reply.

"We have been expecting for you for quite a while. We received a message from Madame B," the old doctor said.

"Unless I am mistaken, I thought I could spend the night here," I said, even though I was not at all sure about it. Nor was I sure why Madame B should have sent me here.

"Yes, or course, Mr X." With this, Dr Mežulis slapped my shoulder and invited me deeper into the building. "Come along and we'll show you to your room. But perhaps you'd first like to take a look at our little undertaking?"

Since it was early afternoon and I had no desire to turn in, I eagerly accepted his offer. With great enthusiasm and pride, the doctor showed me around the territory of the convalescent home with its many buildings. Each one of them was named after an outstanding and mentally unbalanced patient – there were houses named after Anna, Augusts, Marija and Osvalds.

"Who knows, maybe one day you will get one, too," he giggled, but I didn't find it very funny. During our walk through the shady park we kept encountering groups of ladies or gentlemen who, I'd grasped, were not here for a stroll but as patients of the institution.

"Don't worry, they present no danger to society," Dr Mežulis said, as if guessing the train of my thought. "Their delusion, life in the grip of illusions and obsessions – all of these can make life difficult to bear both for themselves and for others. If a person begins to represent danger to himself or others, if he becomes uncontrollable, it may already be too late. Then other kinds of treatment are in order."

"Is Madame B…" I did not finish my question.

"Sorry? What about Madame B?" Dr Mežulis stopped in his tracks, leaning forward.

"Well, I thought, I was under the impression…" I stammered. "I thought that she too would be here."

"Did you?" The doctor looked aside, smoothing his beard. "Interesting, very interesting. But no, Madame B is not here and I was not even aware of her plans to come for a visit."

I mumbled that I must have misunderstood, yet the situation was beginning to worry me. What if Madame B sent me here not because Dr Mežulis was her friend, but because, without being aware of it, I had begun to show signs of some mental illness? Perhaps I was being offered not a place to spend the night before a long journey but an inconspicuous prison?

"No, no, not there!" Dr Mežulis gently touched my elbow, startling me out of my contemplation and, at the intersection of paths, steered me to the right. We once again approached the house where I was to have my room. I gathered that the doctor himself lived on the second floor.

"If you don't mind, I would like to invite you to dinner," he said as we went up the steps to the house. "Of course, once you've settled in and washed. How does in a quarter of an hour sound? Or a bit later?"

I felt a little awkward and asked if my visit would not be an unnecessary bother, but Dr Mežulis dismissed my arguments.

"It is always a pleasure to meet intelligent young people from Riga," he said.

The room where I was going to stay was simple and everything suggested that it, along with the rest of the house, was only recently finished and furnished. I may have even been the first to sleep in that nicely made-up bed. If I hadn't known that I was in a hospital for the insane, this could have passed for a boarding house or sanatorium. It certainly did not look like a place of confinement.

Having washed and combed my hair in front of the mirror, I went out to knock at the door on which a small plaque read "Dr Mežulis".

The door was opened almost immediately, and behind it stood the doctor himself – as if all this time he had been waiting for me on the threshold.

"Kindly come in!" He nudged me ahead of himself and up the stairs. The park had seemed to be always cool and shady, whereas here on the second floor of the New House, it was pleasantly sunny and warm. From a room nearby, the voices of children and a woman were audible – either the doctor's wife or a governess was reading to the children.

Dr Mežulis ushered me into a roomy veranda where I noticed that the table there was set for two.

This must have been the most luxurious dinner I had enjoyed in the last few months. Three different courses were served one after another. First came a clear fish soup, and Dr Mežulis commented that the fish had been caught right there, in the Gauja. Then came steaming potatoes with chanterelle sauce, and the doctor explained that the potatoes were grown at the institution and the chanterelles were gathered in the forests nearby. Finally, along with coffee, we enjoyed lingonberry cake – naturally, made with berries picked in the local swamps and forests. All of this was accompanied by red wine, which alone was not of local origin, and then Dr Mežulis suggested that we move to his study where, sitting in comfortable armchairs and shrouded in fragrant cigar smoke, we each had a glass of cognac.

Even though the hour was not late, my body was overcome by pleasant languor, and my mind was slightly inebriated, which of course is particularly conducive to philosophical contemplation. I decided not to tell Dr Mežulis about my strange dream, yet I did share with him some thoughts that may have been prompted by it.

I must say that even before this I had sometimes felt that the thoughts of all – or nearly all – people in this world are somehow connected by a kind of invisible and very fine web. And as soon as something happens at an intersection of this web, for instance an attack on Franz Ferdinand, news of this travels throughout the entire web, affecting both people nearby and those who live in a faraway corner of the world. Perhaps this invisible web or veil connects not only people but all other living beings or even inanimate objects – trees in the forest, leaves of grass, grains of sand, rocks in a field, the current in the river that ceaselessly flows past us. It can be called different names – soul, spirit, perhaps even some god; however it is not the name that is important, but the great totality of the world where the tiniest bug and the greatest of men have something in common.

"Very interesting," Dr Mežulis said. "By the way, do you know what the very first word you uttered as a child was?"

I found this question somewhat odd, yet I knew the answer because my mother had told me about it more than once. When I was very young, she had often taken me for walks in the forest surrounding the little Ozolkalns lake, so the first word that I learnt to pronounce was "forest".

"I see," the doctor said with a smile. "Are you familiar with William James? No? How about Schopenhauer, Spinoza, Swedenborg? Of course, you are. But do you know what they have in common? It is called panpsychism, and it is the idea that every one of us – and not just human beings – possesses a soul, and this soul, which dwells in the spiritual sphere, not only unites us and makes us similar to each other in a way, but also guides us."

"The thought that someone is guiding me... I have always found it puzzling and I have resisted it," I objected.

"But why are you here then, why are we having this conversation, how did you get here?" Dr Mežulis gave me a sly smile. "Would you really claim that it was your free will that seated you here at my dinner table?"

I found this question confusing, for I have always held the view that every person is in charge of his own fate, and even in seemingly hopeless situations – as evidenced by my recent adventures near Valmiera – one's decisiveness and refusal to lose heart are much more important than a lucky break. Of course, Tidriķis, whom I met there unexpectedly, also had a role in this, but I was quite certain that had he not been there, another opportunity would have come my way.

"For example, your leaving Riga..." the doctor resumed, "was it of your own free will or as a result of circumstance? Of course you made the decision to leave, but let us not forget that there's a war going on. The order to retreat has been given and the army is retreating – and not just the army. So your decision was not determined only by your will, was it? And then? You get to Valmiera. And once again it seems to you that you've been guided by nothing but your will. But tell me, why didn't you go to Cēsis? Or Smiltene? But of course – Madame B, your aunt, lives in Valmiera, and so the decision to opt for Valmiera was dictated not so much by your will as by this circumstance. But can we also say that this was influenced by Madame B and her will?"

"Probably not my getting to Valmiera, but certainly coming here, to you, most directly," I said.

"So you see that you do not always act only in accordance with your will. Which of course does not mean that you are a kind of automaton directed by someone from a distance. Even if Madame B very much wanted for you to visit me but you did not consider it necessary or possible, you would not be sitting here!"

Dr Mežulis peered at me slyly over the top of his glasses.

"Don't get me wrong," he continued. "I have no intention of denying the existence of free will. In my opinion, it has simply been accorded too much significance – either by getting too attached to it or, as it often happens, denying that it exists at all. In both cases, we pretend not to notice that our existence is a much more complicated mechanism and it is not created solely by unidirectional chains of causation."

"Take trees!" He abruptly leaned in my direction, startling me both with this movement and the unexpected mention of trees, for I remembered Madame B's note. "It so happens that in my spare time I enjoy exploring trees. Frankly, I hope to lay the foundations for a new branch of science. For now, I am calling it tree psychology, even though I assume that such a phrase has been used before. What do you think, do trees possess free will?"

"I don't think so," I replied without much hesitation.

"No? And what makes you think that? Let me guess. Could it be the fact that trees are incapable of moving on their own? Wherever they have been planted or are growing, they must remain for the rest of their lives, right? No choice, right?"

"Certainly not," I nodded.

"Yet here we are mistaken," he was grinning now. "We people have an amazing capacity to try to understand and explain everything, using ourselves as a yardstick. It seems that if one of the expressions of freedom for us, people, is the ability to move seemingly independently to wherever we wish, then everything else – be it heavenly bodies, rocks, plants or animals – would also possess such freedom only if they had such an ability. It doesn't even occur to us that our freedom depends not on a more or less purposeful moving about on our part but vice versa – moving is only one of many different expressions of freedom. If I were asked if a rock possesses freedom, I would say, in firm belief, yes, absolutely, and, moreover, to a greater degree than you or I possess it. A rock, unless it is immured somewhere or turned into, say, a stone axe or a headstone, is substantially freer even than the birds and beasts to which we attribute so little agency, we don't even believe them capable of sowing and reaping. The burden of duty, responsibility before oneself and others, hopes for and worries about the future, scruples and pleasant memories about the past – there is no doubt that without it all we would hardly be considered human, yet for our humanity we pay with freedom.

But let us get back to the trees. You see, it is my view that a tree's freedom is something close to ideal – something that we all should strive for. In rocks and minerals, there is already too much freedom – so much that it could easily be confused with indifference, ignorance and insensibility. They say that there are people with a stone instead of a heart, right? But the plant kingdom and trees are in a kind of balance: they are in between the supposedly inanimate minerals and the irrepressibly active living things. It is true, the roots of an oak penetrate the soil exactly in the spot where an acorn has fallen, and there it does not have much choice. Yet it can send out any of its roots in whichever direction it pleases, and this is even more in the case of branches – they can reach up or bend down, they may grow into a pyramid or form a round or quadrangular crown. To us these may seem like minute and unimportant details, but for an oak these decisions, if we can call them that, mean a fulfilment of its life. And each one entails making an important choice!"

Dr Mežulis stroked his white beard. An awkward silence settled in, for I had no idea what to say to the doctor or whether he even expected me to provide some sort of an evaluation of his theories.

"I see that you're tired," he said. "I must apologise if I have worn you out with my reflections. Lately, I haven't had many guests with whom it would be nice to have a chat. There are times when I feel as lonely as a tree. Don't mind me."

I protested that he was certainly not the reason for my fatigue, which was probably the fault of my hike over the last few days followed by his delightful dinner.

"Yes, yes, yes!" Dr Mežulis smiled and patted me on the shoulder. "I know, I know, it's called good manners."

He accompanied me to the first floor and shook my hand by the door. Only then did I notice that two of the fingers on his right hand were crooked and could no longer be straightened. Feeling awkward, I may have drawn back my hand too quickly, for the doctor noticed and said, "So you see that trees are not alone in ageing and turning into gnarled stumps. Time passes and every one of us receives the secret handshake of old age."

It was still quite light outside and I decided to take a little walk before turning in. I traversed the park and, passing overgrown tributary inlets, walked to the Gauja. Curiously the Gauja had been my constant companion on this journey. I went down to the water, found a log that had washed ashore and sat down on it to reflect on my conversation with Dr Mežulis. A little way downstream there were several bonfires, and muffled conversations could be heard, yet I didn't want to get any closer – having no idea who they were. Besides, it was pleasant to remain invisible, blending in with the grassy riverbank with its piles of fallen trees, and imagine that a small fragment of the world could be observed from outside – without participating in it.

This is how Dr Mežulis's trees might look upon the world – without the slightest chance of moving themselves, without causing the slightest suspicion that they see, understand and remember everything. For a moment, it occurred to me that it might be lumbermen by the bonfire, but that surely was a silly idea, since downstream Germans were already in charge and this was not the right time of year to float logs downstream. Suddenly some shots rang out on the opposite side of the river. It was clear that the shooting was taking place a couple of kilometres away, yet panic set in amongst the supposed lumbermen. The bonfires were quickly doused, voices grew excited and a moment later, darkness and silence reigned on the riverbank. Only later did it occur to me that the men must have been scouts preparing to go downriver when it got dark and circle to the rear of the enemy. Carefully feeling my way, I sneaked back to my shelter for the night and was glad not to encounter a living soul in the institution's garden, unless the dark fir trees whose tops were rustling mournfully in the autumn wind could qualify. I couldn't sleep for some time, as all night long the shooting was now closer and then further away.

26 August

I had a horrible dream during my brief sleep. I found myself in a small but opulent theatre. The lights slowly went out and the gold, crystal and red velvet finery sank into darkness. The curtain opened and the performance began, only it wasn't theatre, opera or operetta – more like the moving pictures. In contrast to those, however, the horrible scenes that unfolded were coloured and accompanied by a horrendous noise.

In fact, these were not even scenes, for the entire stage was filled with a huge face with sunken cheeks, bared teeth and a mocking expression. It was Death itself who, in the guise of a woman fresh out of the grave and covered with dust, addressed those present. Her bones were protruding through wilted flesh and it was hard to tell where the remnants of her rotted clothing ended and what had once been flesh began. Amongst the audience were many military officers and, finding the horrible phantom unbearable, they began to shoot at it. Yet each one of the shots had an opposite effect on the dead visage from what could have been expected. For an instant it was engulfed in flames, but, once the fire died down, Death had become even bigger. Its mouth ridiculed the attempts to shoot it and jeered at the panicking audience.

Oppressive heat was emanating from the stage, and Death shouted that she would throw pieces of her flesh into the audience and those it hit would have to die. The spectators jumped to their feet, stumbled, fell, crawled chaotically over each other, but Death just raised her arm and tossed a handful of flesh, and then another and another. Those hit by the rotten flesh did not die immediately. From the yellowish-brown piles of remains emerged beetles who seemed to be made of precious stones lit from the inside; they carefully looked the doomed victims up and down to memorise them and then took wing and returned to the stage. At the moment when a heavy projectile of rot hit me and I fell down, I did not lose all reason but thrust my hand into it and pulled out the shiny little monster. It kept wriggling, trying to get away from my hand, but I held on to it, prised it open and began to dismantle it piece by piece. Inside, it had a mess of fine pinions, wires and levers, at which I tore without mercy till I found the centre where on a kind of a watch face I saw my own name. After I'd turned one of the pinions, the name disappeared and I realised that I was saved. Death on stage continued to cackle, shots were heard from all around, pieces of dead flesh flew about as did the mechanical beetles, but I paid it all no heed, for I knew that nothing could harm me. I began to elbow my way to the exit and soon woke up.

It was still dark outside, but I decided to not wait for dawn and not say goodbye to Dr Mežulis. Having dressed quickly and gathered my modest belongings, I cautiously opened the window and stepped out on to the white, dew-covered grass. I didn't want to bang the door and risk waking the doctor or his servant. I had no desire to run into either of them.

"Goodbye," a voice gave me a start and I almost cried out. In the semi-darkness, I could see someone standing under the fir tree – someone whom I had actually taken for a tree. It turned out to be one of the two women I had encountered when I first arrived: the one who had showed me the way to the New House.

"Goodbye," I gave a restrained reply and hurried on my way.

28 November

After arriving in Valka, I abandoned my journal for quite a while. The last few months had been full of worrisome events and, despite my recent plans, wishes and convictions, I too was dragged into the maelstrom. The fact that great changes were afoot was clear from the beginning of October: Bolsheviks behaved like masters of the situation and, without any restraint, urged the toppling of the existing powers. Meanwhile our own Latvian Soldiers Union and its newspaper *News of the Times*, which came out in Cēsis, called for adopting a Latvian constitution and establishing our own independent statehood. But the National Union lacked both the impudence of the Bolsheviks and a proper grip on power; more and more soldiers were listening to Bolshevik agitation and they now had a sizeable army. Members of the National Union were even forced to escape from Cēsis to Valka after the Bolsheviks' plans to kill them came to light. It could well have happened, even though some thought it unlikely. What followed the Bolshevik revolution defied imagination.

The prevailing mood was grim, not to say hopeless. Against this background of despair, our Latvian inability to achieve unity of purpose prevailed and we failed to resist Bolshevik designs. Even before the Bolshevik revolution, Estonians had managed to get the posts of regional judges and commissioners for their own in place of Russians, and that alone was an achievement. Something was not quite right with the Latvians, I thought to myself. We are too compliant and submissive; we keep quiet, tolerate and refrain from resisting. And all the dreams of the National Union were therefore nothing more than a waste of words. If anything remained of the army, the Bolsheviks made sure that it was damaged or destroyed. Officers were demoted to rank and file and, unless they were able to escape, they had to do the heaviest and most unpleasant chores. I heard that some were made to clean and take out the latrines, while others were put on menial duties such as fetching water.

Anyone could become an officer in the Bolshevik army, yet it seemed that dumb NCOs were particularly favoured, and some of them even began calling themselves generals. Bolsheviks were busy setting up reliable land councils, which did not hesitate to take under their control the local governments both in towns and the countryside. Those who tried to resist or even voice their objections to the new order faced immediate retribution: sentences were pronounced without involving any courts – they could not be appealed and meant execution. In the face of such terror, Latvian dreams of freedom and of liberating themselves from foreign overlords seemed irresponsible, naive and childish. You cannot hope to be taken for a fearsome warrior if you're constantly on the run and creeping around.

I woke up early as usual. By now I was used to waking up at four or five. The stove had burnt out quickly, the room had turned really cold and, even though both doors and windows were tightly locked, dankness seeped in from the hidden corners and cracks. I don't mean to suggest I started to wake early simply because of the colder weather (or even my increasing hunger, as it was getting harder to find food). Usually I woke up quite well rested and could not get back to sleep because of some immediate and irrepressible thoughts: How are my parents were doing? Are they still at the estate or did they decide to leave at the last moment? And what's happening in Riga, what has happened to my room? Where is the soloist K singing these days – the one I met not so long ago? And what fate has befallen Tidriķis and Alberts?

But this time it wasn't the usual musings that kept me from sleeping in. At first it seemed to me as if something had hit the roof with a muffled thud. I opened my eyes. As usual, I was sleeping in the kitchen in front of the stove – I considered heating the whole empty apartment both impossible and senseless. What I had thought to be something thudding against the roof turned out to be cautious steps on the veranda staircase on the first floor. I could have been mistaken, but I thought I heard some voices. Yes, now the steps were clearly audible – a pebble or clump of sand made a scraping sound under the weight of the strangers, and the frosted grass crunched. It sounded like there were many of them.

Later it seemed to me as if I had noticed a dark outline behind the glass of the big hallway door, but it could not have been the case, because outside there was still the darkness of night and not even a hint of morning in the sky.

At that moment I woke up – in reality. I did not sleep in the kitchen; there was no hallway door with a glass; I was in bed on the second floor. And I knew that if steps were heard from the uninhabited ground floor of the house, a stranger had come in.

A few heavy pieces of birch firewood had been left in the box by the stove. Nearby was a small axe, which I used to make kindling. The Smith & Wesson given to me by Tidriķis was right there, under my pillow. That was the entirety of my modest arsenal. Various plans of action were flashing through my mind. Should I wait for the uninvited visitors by the door, then fling it open and surprise them right here, at the top of the stairs with a surprise attack worthy of Clausewitz? Shoot, beat and throw the pieces of wood all at once in an effort to propel them down the steep staircase? And what next?

All my momentarily conceived plans were complicated by an unpleasant circumstance. Living in Valka under conditions of deceptive peace, I had become spoiled and in the habit of taking off my boots and undressing before going to bed, so presently my clothes were next to me on a chair and my boots were on the floor in a corner.

I carefully slipped out of bed, quietly gathered my belongings and, walking on tiptoe and trying to avoid squeaky boards, scrambled for the balcony door. The door was the most difficult obstacle to my plan, for it was very hard to open and made much noise. Even though I understood that I could not lose a minute, I gathered all my strength and pushed the door open as slowly as possible and almost without a sound. Outside it was cloudy and cold, there was a light drizzle, and that immediately revitalised me. I paused to listen for the presence of strangers in the garden and then threw down my things, crawled over the railing and slid down into an overgrown flower bed. Inside the house, I heard steps and voices. Having concluded that there was no one on the first floor, they went upstairs. I scurried away, squeezing out between the wall of the barn and a growth of shrubs, and ran down to Varžupīte. I'd scouted this escape route beforehand, even though I didn't know whether I would ever have to use it. On the riverbank, I put on my clothes and boots, and was ready to be on my way.

Later I heard that Bolsheviks had been searching for "deserters" and taking them prisoner. Fortunately this raid was not very successful, mainly because of their ineptitude, bad reconnaissance, boastfulness, drinking and chaotic behaviour. As I was told later, the previous evening some Bolsheviks had been bragging at the local inn that in the coming nights they were planning to round up all the "elements".

At sunrise, I was already quite a way out of Valka and walking towards Dorpat.

I had no inkling that the enemy were once again hot on my heels, bringing devastation with them: the new year had barely begun when the German army launched an attack along the entire front, taking Polotsk, Dvinsk and soon thereafter also Cēsis, Valmiera and Valka.

13 April 1918

Still no news from home. For almost a month I've been staying with Prince G on his estate near Moscow along with Alberts, whom I met in Moscow, and another two young officers, Bērziņš and Riekstiņš. It has been a while since I've recorded anything, so I must briefly explain how we got here and how it came about that my mood and train of thought have significantly changed.

After reaching Moscow by train, I tried to get in touch with nationally minded or at least Bolshevik-opposing people and correctly supposed that I would find such people amongst the former employees of the committee responsible for caring and providing for refugees, which had now been taken over and disbanded by the Bolsheviks. I met one of them, Zariņš, and here I have to mention a trivial matter, which, upon our meeting seemed just an amusing curiosity, and yet I have, to this day, been unable to put it out of my mind. At times it triggers a rather peculiar reverie:, his handshake, it was strong yet unusual, because the small finger of his right hand was rigid and crooked. Of course it made me think of Dr Mežulis with his unusual theories of tree psychology and age-stiffened fingers. Zariņš promised to get me together with several patriots who, in defiance to the Bolshevik threat and at constant risk to their own lives, were laying the groundwork for an independent state they could call their own. They were doing this together "with our mutual friends" (*at that moment I failed to understand that he was talking about the English*). To my great surprise, the main one of those saviours of our homeland praised by Zariņš turned out to be the most sceptical of my friends, namely Alberts.

"It is human nature to change one's thoughts and beliefs," Alberts responded to my amazement, and shrugged his shoulders. "At the time I thought it a completely foolish and hopeless undertaking and, frankly, would have continued to think this way if I hadn't found out that we weren't alone in caring about Latvian independence. Of course, it was obvious why the English were interested in this matter, but why should I care about that? To me, it was simply a business relationship."

My views were "fatefully" transformed by this meeting, what Alberts said and what I had experienced during my long walk. The old sceptic and pursuer of self-interest stepped aside in Finland or some other safe place, and a new ardour flared up within me. I was very familiar with it, despite my habitual disavowals. Perhaps it was this that had prevented me from forming a more or less lasting romantic relationship with the fair sex. Next to fearlessness, there was always the allure of risky ventures, and the more hopeless the venture seemed, the greater the allure. Often I had experienced failures or fiascos, if you will, but that was another good reason to wallow in misery and contemplate man's fate as endless suffering. And yet here was an adventure that apparently had already reached its peak in hopelessness.

Thus, with Alberts's blessing, we began our "spy time" in Moscow and our activities in Boris Savinkov's Association for the Protection of Homeland and Freedom.

Our greatest achievement was the pretence that the Latvian riflemen were demobilising after Germany and Russia signed a peace treaty in Brest. The treaty provided for the demobilisation of the army, yet the Bolshevik government did not want to observe this undertaking; it wanted to keep the reliable unit of riflemen. It was a well-known fact that many riflemen no longer wanted to bear arms. Pretending to act in the name of the National Union, we announced that it would help the riflemen return home. In order to make everything look official, we even issued a call for the riflemen to report to us, and requested donations to cover their living costs and their journey home. When we notified the regiments, the riflemen were ecstatic about demobilisation and we were able to send off several formations (with at least two hundred riflemen in each) to Siberia right under the noses of the Bolsheviks, away from the obligation to obey Bolshevik orders. We also managed to send trainloads of arms and munitions straight from the front in a direction not favoured by the Bolsheviks. I found out the intended final destinations of these trains well in advance so that people we trusted at these destinations could send telegrams declaring it would not be possible to accept trains carrying cargoes of this kind and that therefore they should be dispatched further to the east. Given the pervasive chaos in Russia at the time, it is likely that more than one formation and its guns and munitions would be roaming the wastes of Siberia for quite some time.

Despite all the post-revolutionary chaos, we had attracted the Bolsheviks' attention. Very soon after grabbing power, at the beginning of December, the Bolsheviks had established their "Extraordinary Commission" or the Cheka, which was charged with the task of waging a ruthless war against various counter-revolutionary "elements", which obviously included us. The last train of "demobilised" riflemen even ran into serious problems. The riflemen were not willing to give up their rifles and arrived at the designated station well armed. But there we were surprised by Chekists: arriving in several trucks and equipped with a machine gun, they demanded that the riflemen put down their arms. The riflemen were not ready to give in so easily and were about to begin a senseless skirmish. Luckily, we managed to calm them down and finally they were forced to return to their regiment. Alberts and I managed to escape by the skin of our teeth, whereas Bērziņš and Riekstiņš were arrested by the Cheka as the main troublemakers. Only through the interference of Colonel B did we manage to free them, but it was clear that there would be no safe haven for us in either Moscow or some other large city, and thus we had to go underground for a while.

With help from Colonel B and our good acquaintance Marshak, chief of the criminal police in Moscow, we all ended up here at the country estate of Prince G, where they even found quite well-paid jobs for us. At the beginning of the year, the Bolsheviks had plundered the estate, carrying off anything that was possible to move through the deep snow and breaking, burning or abandoning whatever proved to be too heavy to carry. They had beaten up the estate's factor and made him go down the steep and iced-over slope in his underwear to get water for their horses. The old man apparently became sick and took to his bed for almost a month, after which this episode appeared to have left a profound and irreversible effect on his psyche.

Soon after the Brest treaty was concluded, the prince's son, Fyodor Pavlovich, returned to this scene of devastation. He was a decent and modest man who was concerned not so much about his property as Russia's tragic fate. He was a brave officer, several times wounded in battle, recipient of St George's sword and the order of Vladimir, and not long before the Bolshevik revolution he had lost his right leg.

He paid us a decent salary for guarding the estate – two hundred and fifty roubles to each of us, in addition to warm shelter and free food, not to mention the free vodka made by the poor factor, who is a real master of this trade.

We would drink quite a few glasses while we sat with Fyodor Pavlovich by his fireplace during those dark evenings, yet I have to say that none of us were ever drunk. The drink that was brought in from the cold and poured into glasses of all shapes and sizes (whatever had survived the destructive fury of the Bolsheviks) was pleasantly warming and fully justified the link established in so many languages between distillation and the spiritual world: "spiritus", "spirutuose", "spirits", "спирт".

As we sat by the fire, the sitting room's semi-darkness was only dispersed by the orange flames, and it seemed that some unifying spirit was flowing into our veins, connecting us through invisible ties with other men also sitting in various parts of Russia and trying to spot some sign of hope or meaning in the near and distant future – the same hope and significance Bolshevik power, having lost their support through its madness, was trying systematically to eradicate. At these moments, a peculiar sense of togetherness that not only united – or so it seemed to me – those who were living in the here and now but also built a bridge across the abyss of time and allowed us to imagine how ancient Greeks might have tried to find answers to unanswerable questions in long conversations, or how the first Christians might have contemplated their impending fate in the catacombs of ancient Rome.

Of course, I couldn't help recalling the unusual meeting with Madame B and her theory about the macrocosm's influence on each of our microcosms. Even though I'm inclined not to believe in such supernatural phenomena, I have always believed that our inner world, like the one surrounding us, is full of things that are currently inexplicable and incomprehensible to the human mind. And who knows – perhaps there really exists an all-embracing element, soul or spirit, which man can, for the time being, sense as a barely perceptible draft or glance. Both Madame B with her "grand truths" and Dr Mežulis with his faith in the psyche of trees, plants and even rocks would then turn out to be right in a way, although I'm convinced that as soon as this common spirit or soul is discovered, none of the existing vocabulary will match the true composition and essence of this phenomenon. In the history of mankind and scientific discoveries there is no lack of such instances. Didn't we believe for a long time that the earth under our feet was flat instead of being a ball and likewise, that the sun was circling around the earth and not the other way round?

Every time such discoveries are made, we not only change our perception of the world, but also the way we think and talk about it. Who knows, perhaps we are once more on the brink of similar transformations? And perhaps the Bolsheviks know or sense this too, which would explain their blind hatred and whey they're trying to destroy everything that up till now has been respected, venerated and held sacred, yet not been fully understood. These horrible atrocities the Russians have been inflicting on priests, monks and nuns of the Orthodox faith which seemed such an integral part of their nature, where did such hatred come from? I don't believe in Madame B's horoscopes and Age of Aquarius, but perhaps there is some hidden explanation in physics or some other science? Could it be astronomy instead of astrology? Could it be that the movements of heavenly bodies have a varying influence on our movements here on Earth? After all, they say that when the moon is full, dogs become particularly ferocious and madmen particularly mad. And I remember well: very soon after the revolution, exactly at the time when the

Bolsheviks began their wild rampage, a full moon was seen in the sky over St Petersburg.

I must have dozed off, warmed by the fireplace and vodka, and was brought to full consciousness by these lines of poetry recited by Fyodor Pavlovich:

"Мужайтеся, безвинные страдальцы –
Лишь дайте мне добраться до Москвы,
А там Борис расплатится во всем..."[1]

I think it must have been Pushkin. Fyodor Pavlovich got up, bid us goodnight and went to bed. For quite a while we heard the clacking sound intermittently made against the parquet of the hallways by his wooden leg and the walnut cane. Finally, some door banged shut and silence settled in. I remained at the fireplace for some time, watching the flames. Wherever the fire touched the wood, it soon turned to coal and then collapsed in ashes – just like everything else, including us humans. Both Fyodor Pavlovich and I must have got into poetic reverie tonight.

20 April

A fantastic morning: warm and sunny, the snow was melting, lumps of it were falling off branches, and birds were singing on the park trees. "The titmouse is chiselling a blade," this is how my mother used to describe the song of the titmouse to me when I was a little boy, and the memory turned my thoughts back to "our" estate and to my parents.

Sheltered and in the sun, it was so warm in front of the manor house that from early in the morning it was possible to sit on the terrace without a coat. I sat in a wicker chair, smoked my first morning cigarette and drank coffee, the

---

1 Courage, you guiltless sufferers –
  Just let me get to Moscow,
  And Boris there will pay for all...

grimness of my thoughts in complete contrast with the radiant blue sky, the springtime mood of the birds and the white of the unmelted snow. From the front of the manor one could see far below to the lake, which was still covered by a thick layer of ice. And my mood only appeared to be matched by some large black birds – crows or possibly jackdaws – squawking at each other from gnarled branches.

Before being interrupted by the memory flash about my parents and the estate, my mind had kept returning to the dream I'd had during the night.

In my dream, I was walking along an overgrown riverbank. The snow had melted and the ice thawed, or perhaps it was late autumn. It might have been the upper reaches of the Gauja or some other river. A brown, soundless current carried torn-off leaves, branches and various refuse. Looking into the water, I suddenly saw someone observing me from the opposite bank. There was Alberts, motionless, wearing a long, white winter camouflage coat and looking at me. I felt I had so much to tell him, I had to tell him something important, but for some reason, I could not speak. I could not get out a single word. So we stared at each other in complete silence, and then Alberts turned, ostensibly to walk along his bank, and I saw that his head was split in two – between the two parts, the back of the head and face, there was a big empty space that one could see through, and the head was held together by an iron band, tightened by some large screws. I do not remember any more, because I woke up in horror. And all morning I was torturing myself, trying to remember what it was that I wanted to tell Alberts.

As if this weren't enough, I had this sudden pang about my mother and father. Once, when there were just the two of us, Father said to me that he could never survive Mother's death. Yet, he said, he could never do himself in either. "I am too weak for either outcome," he said. "I could neither live nor die."

76

I feel desperate thinking that something bad might have happened with my mother and father. I have long since abandoned any illusions that I may have had concerning human nature and, as I've been forced to find out, the worst that can happen usually does. At the same time, I cannot imagine being present at the moment of my mother's or my father's death, where I would see with my own eyes how a person dear to me steps over the threshold of existence and turns into nothing. Over these years, I have seen death over and over again, and I know that it is no being, place or entrance to another form of existence. It is exactly like fire in the fireplace. Only an empty space remains after the fire has consumed the firewood. And a dead person is just an empty space. Frozen to death in winter's bitter cold, dismembered, face distorted by the last gasp, eyes wide open, buried in mud, burnt to ash or carefully tended to and laid in a coffin – it makes no difference what dead people look like, for the only possible feeling in their presence is the realisation that they are no more and never will exist again. Only a month into the Great War in the autumn of 1914, this empty space was already two hundred and sixty thousand wide. In the battle of Verdun, which lasted almost an entire year, this void expanded by seven hundred thousand, and now the estimated death toll is up to ten million. That's ten million empty spaces where before there were that many people. Or am I wrong? What if it's not just an empty space that remains?

The horrible dream made me think about all of this. Alberts was obviously dead – no one could survive with such holes in one's head, screwed together or not. And yet he moved, stared in my direction, seemed to wait for me to say something, and continued to be human.

It's probably wrong to think like this, but I do hope that I'm not there when my parents' time comes. And I also hope that this would be their wish too. And that they will never have to wonder about my own fate or be the first to get a death notice. And I hope that they won't experience any pain or torment, but die in peace.

My grim ruminations were interrupted and I was startled to find that Alberts had shown up (alive and well, of course). Before my eyes the dreamscape was still very real, and yet there he stood on the terrace – with that crooked smile of his and always ready with some witticism. I didn't tell him anything about my dream. Although he was even more of a sceptic and cynic than I was, who knows how he would have responded to someone who'd seen him not quite alive and not exactly dead.

"Good morning, good morning!" he greeted me merrily. "The sun is practically walking the earth. Almost makes one feel like multiplying."

This is how I remembered him a couple of years later upon learning that Alberts had fallen at Perekop. A grenade had torn off half his head.

23 April

Out on the terrace this morning, Fyodor Pavlovich and I began a discussion about time. In this regard, he's a rather traditionally minded person and, in our conversation, even came to the conclusion that if we had no clocks and watches, we would barely be able to talk about time.

For the sake of an argument, I put forward a quite extravagant theory which had occurred to me just as I woke up a few days previously. What if time turned out to be not a linear segment or a vector but a vertical pierced through space, which is stacked layer upon layer – like pancakes or, more precisely, rings of an onion or a tree? Time would not be one arrow directed from the past to the future through the present but hundreds, thousands, millions and billions of such movements, which could pierce the chronologically stacked space at different forces and velocities. And that would mean that, at least theoretically, greater or smaller shifts in time could take place in space – for instance, Fyodor Pavlovich's present day could place itself next to my present day and this very moment, but it would not mean that his present day was objectively mine, and by the same token, it could be my next day or yesterday or some even more distant time. Thus in the subjective "today" of any person, an almost unlimited number of times from the recent or more distant past could meet the present. That, amongst other things, could help with understanding such phenomena as the supposedly mistaken conviction that the here and now has already been experienced. The "predictions" of future events might thus acquire a solid rational basis. Not to mention dreams.

"Ah, you should turn to science," Fyodor Pavlovich said with a grin, "instead of running around the world in a uniform."

Fyodor Pavlovich's readings served as an impetus for this conversation. During the time we spent at his estate, he periodically wanted to read out loud excerpts from his biography, which he was in the process of writing. Although it would be an exaggeration to attribute to it any great literary quality, I must admit that Fyodor Pavlovich has a gift for storytelling, with an admirable ability to observe and remember seemingly minor but distinct details.

When Fyodor Pavlovich had finished reading, I asked if he had ever thought about whether memories in our consciousness only form when we put them into words – either orally or in writing. In other words, we can only call things "memories" once they've been narrated either to ourselves or to someone else.

"This sounds interesting," Fyodor Pavlovich said, "yet I don't really understand what your point is."

I explained that the formation of memories was probably comparable to our colour perception. As has been known for several centuries, light does not have a colour: there are just light waves of different lengths. When they enter our eyes simultaneously, we see white. But when, after the refraction of light rays at various angles, only the waves of certain lengths enter our eyes, we conclude that an object is yellow or pink, or some other colour. Our colour perception depends on how our eyes work. It can be said that objectively nothing has colour. Every one of us creates colours, and so do mammals, birds and bugs. And it doesn't even mean that two people sitting next to each other, looking at a field of snow or the blue sky and agreeing that the snow is white and the sky blue, see the same thing.

"Yes, that's clear and well known." A note of impatience could be heard in Fyodor Pavlovich's voice. "But what does it have to do with my memories?"

"Everything," I replied. The "objective reality" surrounding man is in a certain sense similar to light – it has no properties. It is neither good nor evil; it possesses nothing of what people ascribe to what is happening around them. We all tend to imagine ourselves as the centre of the world and its phenomena. We seem to find ourselves in the very centre of one of those medieval maps where the centre was either Jerusalem or Constantinople. We fancy that everything revolves around us and that the world without our presence would be something entirely different. It could even be that way if, at the same time, we could observe the world from outside, without being in it. Yet it is impossible. And the world without us would, in all likelihood, be the same as with us in it.

We make an event or a thing special only when we think about it and verbalise our thoughts. Instead of just letting our glance glide across a frozen lake or rest with birds perched on tree branches, we must think, Ah, a lake, and the ice is still rather thick, and spring is in the air. And at that exact moment, the lake stops being just some lake, or the growth of trees the same as hundreds of thousands of others, for they have become part of us. We have become aware of them in a most primitive fashion and yet managed to retain that awareness in our minds, perhaps in order to some day transform it into a poem, musical composition or simply a memory. But then we have to return to what we've seen, heard or perceived some other way, paying attention to this or that detail – in other words, we have to process our experience so that it can seem as authentic and real to us as possible.

"Just think," I said. "If this very evening we sat at our desks and recalled our morning conversation and everything around us, we would certainly end up with two very different descriptions."

Fyodor Pavlovich considered this for a moment.

"But then it follows," he said, "that there is no objective reality?"

"Not exactly," I objected. "It's just that for a large part, it remains imperceptible, unnoticed and unimportant to us. You of course will not deny that we find ourselves on a spherical planet..."

"...called Earth," Fyodor Pavlovich concluded.

"No, no, here I got you!" I smiled. "Tell me, if there were no one who knew the word 'Earth', could we then say that there is no such planet?"

"I see," Fyodor Pavlovich said pensively. "But then there would be no us either!"

"Also not true. For who says that 'Earth' is the only word with which to name this planet? It could also be called... I don't know – 'Moon', for instance. And would our planet then cease to exist?"

Fyodor Pavlovich did not reply. The wind brought the heavy puffing of an engine and a long whistle from across the lake.

"So some sort of objective reality probably does exist. The only problem is that we tend to live each in our own subjectively perceived world created in our own consciousness."

"It's rather depressing," Fyodor Pavlovich said. "Particularly when you're forced to admit that God no longer has a place in it all."

He uttered this with chagrin and even anger, and it was equally obvious that for a substantial part of his life such a thought wouldn't have entered his mind. I didn't ask what might have changed his views, but assumed that the old prince must have been religious and educated his son in the Christian spirit.

"So all that we can hold on to, is space and time," he let out a mirthless laugh.

At that moment, I had no idea that very soon this conversation would appear to sink into the distant past where it could slumber for all eternity.

Around two in the afternoon, the caretaker's shaggy dog began to bark hysterically. Some strange rumbling was heard in the alley leading to the manor from the direction of the highway, getting louder. Unsure of what it might mean, we assumed positions on the balcony and at the windows in the front part of the building, loaded our weapons and prepared to defend it. Fyodor Pavlovich too pulled out his Nagant revolver.

An automobile emerged from the alley and proceeded to clamber up the hill to the manor. Inside it sat two men, tightly wrapped in scarves and overcoats for warmth, their eyes protected by goggles. It stopped by the front door and both got out. Since they didn't look aggressively inclined, I walked out to greet them.

To my great surprise, I recognised one of the men as Colonel B. Reddened by the cold, his moustache frosted over, he greeted me like an old acquaintance, although we'd only met on a few occasions. The man who had sat by the steering wheel was a stranger to me. Without much delay, I invited both in and introduced them to Fyodor Pavlovich. Even though the day was sunny, the wind had been blustery, and the two visitors were happy to accept the invitation to warm themselves by the fireplace and have a drink.

And then the colonel revealed the reason for their visit. Surprisingly, the reason turned out to be me. Being fully aware of the success Alberts and I had had in bamboozling the Bolsheviks, he had an offer to make.

"It should in no way be considered an order," he said. "For I am not in a position to give you orders or you in a position to comply with them. That's a done deal. So please consider it a request instead. And also an offer."

Yet first he discreetly tried to find out if Fyodor Pavlovich could be trusted and if I did not have any objections to discuss political issues in his presence. I confirmed to the colonel that I counted on the prince completely and had nothing I wished to hide from him.

Yet the prince was surprised by the colonel's offer – possibly even more so than I. To cut a long story short, I was expected to cross the frontlines back to Vidzeme, visit Valka, Valmiera and Riga, and then investigate things in all of Kurzeme, way up to Ventspils, find out the situation and then report on what I'd managed to find out and observe.

"Believe me, the day will come when the liberation of our country will begin, and the intelligence you have gathered will be of the greatest importance," the colonel said. "Of course you will earn a decent reward for this undertaking." And he mentioned a truly handsome amount of money.

"When would you be ready to leave?" he asked.

Without giving it a second thought, I answered that I could go the following day. I asked if I really had to go alone, to which the colonel gave a strict "yes".

Although I was immediately conscious of all the hardships and danger that I could expect on this adventure, I also experienced an overwhelming sense of joy. Its main source was the awareness that I would return to places dear to me and that I could once again see my mother and father. I was also happy that this would bring an end to this senseless sitting around in one place. Even though Fyodor Pavlovich was a hospitable host and a pleasant conversationalist, life on the estate had become routine, from time to time even upsetting me with its sheer boredom. To disabuse the colonel and Fyodor Pavlovich of any mistaken view they may have had of me, I said that I was not taking this mission for the money. Nor did I have any great illusions regarding the independence of my country – it's just that I am impetuous by nature and I like to get involved in risky undertakings.

The colonel then gave me more detailed instructions along with the promised amount of money and new documents: from that moment on, I was correspondent L of the newspaper *Раннее утро* (since I think I already wrote about the insignificance of my "real" personality a few days ago, changing my name seemed only natural to me). The colonel wouldn't listen when Fyodor Pavlovich and I suggested that he stay the night, and left that very evening.

That was our last encounter, as a few months later the Bolsheviks arrested the colonel, charged him with conspiracy and had him executed.

As this was my last evening at the estate, Fyodor Pavlovich decided to organise a modest feast for us. A pike from the nearby lake was put on the table, along with pickled apples, cucumbers and mushrooms in brine and, of course, sauerkraut, boiled unpeeled potatoes and many other simple dishes, which were like delicacies in those tumultuous times. All washed very nicely with a well-known vodka of local provenance.

We were not in the mood for philosophical conversation that evening. In a way, I really had "become a different person" and was preparing for the task the colonel had given me, while Fyodor Pavlovich seemed to be slightly chagrined that I would no longer entertain him with my company.

In spite of having eaten a prolonged dinner and relaxed by the fireplace, I found it difficult to sleep. I kept leafing through a frayed pre-war issue of *Dress and Vanity Fair*, studying gentlemen's fashions and chuckling at the appropriateness of the magazine title. "Vanity Fair" – that was exactly what the pre-war world could be called. We had lived our lives full of hope and illusions, considering how we appeared to others to be more important than how we really were. Only five years had passed, but so many masks had fallen and we'd discovered so much that is unpleasant about human nature. And who knows, perhaps this world would finally wake up purer and better after all of this destruction? Of course not in the way the Bolsheviks imagined and promised in their leaflets – one thing was for sure: their rule was doomed; it had no future and wouldn't last long.

24 April

The morning was overcast and chilly. I deliberately got up early to try and avoid prolonged goodbyes, yet it seemed that all the residents of the estate, including the dog, rooster and both of the caretaker's cats, had decided to resist this attempt and managed to greet me. Alberts, Bērziņš and Riekstiņš were also up, not to mention Fyodor Pavlovich, who waited for me in the dining room, impeccably dressed as usual, as if he had never gone to bed.

In honour of my departure, old Yefrosinya had cooked thick pancakes, which were supposed to be eaten with cloudberry jam, yet no one had much of an appetite. Conversation was lagging at the breakfast table. I could tell that Alberts and both of his comrades were a little envious of my unexpected task and would have loved to replace me or at least accompany me. When I light-heartedly mentioned this, they tried their best to infer that this was far from their minds.

The goodbyes between my comrades and me were brief yet heartfelt; it was clear that, like myself, they accepted that we would probably never see each other again. Only the parting from Fyodor Pavlovich took longer. When

I eventually threw my knapsack over my shoulder and reached the front stairs, he caught up with me and handed me a large parcel.

"Take it – it may come in handy next winter if not in this," he said. "One just like it saved my life one winter night in 1914. Who knows where the bayonet would have hit if the German could have seen me better in the semi-darkness and snow."

The parcel contained a white canvas camouflage over-coat. It was very peculiar to receive such a present intended for winter already in the spring, but I knew it would be impolite to refuse. I later remembered that I'd seen the white coat somewhere else: in my dream of dead Alberts. This very real coat in my possession did not feel like a happy association, and I comforted myself with the thought that it could only be coincidence (not at all a fateful one).

Fyodor Pavlovich kindly offered to drive me the two kilometres to the station, but I firmly refused. I wanted to look at the surrounding countryside one more time, for in all likelihood I would never have a chance to return here again.

The last experience relating to Fyodor Pavlovich's estate took place at the end of the path at the forest's edge. Some distance away, I could see smoke rising and hear axes chopping. Under the factor's supervision, two very old workers had cut down some trees. Branches crackled in the bonfire, bright yellow and orange-red wood chippings were strewn across the white snow. One of the trunks was particularly broad and walking by I noticed that it had many dozens of rings in the cross section.

I couldn't get this out of my mind as I walked to the railway station or even when I boarded the train and started travelling towards Pskov. Telegraph poles glided past the window and gradually, in the rhythm of the clanking wheels, I recalled both the conversation with Dr Mežulis and my little argument with Fyodor Pavlovich when, by the manor-house fireplace, I told him my theory on the possible relationship between time and space. It was perfectly clear that regardless of whether we compare the location of events in time to cards, pancakes, onion layers or tree rings, we're describing hypothetical intersections in which our movement through time pierces through the sequential reality of space and, at least theoretically, allows one to be at the same place at different times and at the same time in two or more places.

As I had predicted, I never returned to the estate again. Only many years later did I learn that not long after I left, the Bolsheviks arrested the prince and promptly executed him. They'd later wanted to set up a sanatorium in the ransacked estate, but during the Second World War it had been set on fire while the German army was moving on Moscow. Then the ruins were cleared away.

III. PHOTOGRAPHS

The army of Kaiser's Germany constructed the narrow-gauge railroad along the seashore during the First World War in 1916 in order to transport munitions and soldiers. After the war and the establishment of an independent Latvian state in 1918, it was gradually made suitable for civilian use.

For several decades, a train travelled daily between Ventspils and Mazirbe, and one can only try to imagine how every morning, right here behind the clump of bushes and the overgrown viga, where the best chanterelles grow, you could hear the engine's whistle and the clatter of the wheels. For the residents of the seaside villages it was the main means of transportation both from house to house and to the city and back. The little train, which moved so slowly that one could jump on and off even between stations, continued to chug along the entire period Latvia was independent, during the Second World War and up to the beginning of the 1960s.

Then, as the Cold War escalated, the Kurzeme seaside turned into one of the most carefully watched and better guarded borders of the USSR. The narrow-gauge was liquidated, rails torn out of the ground and replaced by a gravel road. The railroad workers were replaced by Soviet border guards with trained dogs; heavy guns were cemented in the dunes and turned against the coast of Sweden; rockets were brought over; tank shooting ranges and radio spying towers were built. A new, completely different life began for the local residents of the Liv villages. All of a sudden they found themselves in a kind of reservation, which the rest of the residents of Latvia and the entire Soviet Union could enter only with special permits. Some of the villagers began to work salting fish at the fish-processing cooperative "Lenin's Way"; the little red church was turned into the clubhouse of the young pioneer camp of the Ventspils Commercial Port and the large inn into a post office, dairy, library and the municipal executive committee.

For a large section of the shore, fishing was totally forbidden and one could use the beach only during daylight hours – at night, the sand was harrowed so that the border guards could immediately notice any footprints. Of course there was good reason for the authorities' concern: winds and storms kept washing ashore evidence of the imperialist order that was quite different from the Soviet one. Empty, sometimes half-full bottles of bourgeois whisky and decadent gin, beer cans that had lost their fulfilment, unreasonably cheerful plastic lighters, lone sneakers – all of these seemed to represent half-extinct evidence of Captain Grant's existence, and cries for help bleached by the salt of the sea, sun and wind.

For several decades this constituted everyday life on the coast: elderly ladies picking berries scared to death in the forest by Soviet armoured cars driving on manoeuvres or tanks that, with kind permission from the officers, sometimes helped to pull out a car stuck in the mud. Now it has become part of the area's folklore, just like the tales of obstinate Liv kings and the lost narrow-gauge train.

[drawing]

In the city, we printed all the photographs found in the memory card (with the exception of the video recording, of course) on to A4 paper. Now, back in the countryside, we decided to find the spots from where they were taken or the objects featured in the pictures. We had no real idea how it could help us find out about the photographer, his intentions or the circumstances in which they were taken.

"Perhaps if we stand in the exact same spot and look in the same direction we'll be able to feel something," we mused.

"They say that even places and inanimate objects have memory," we pondered.

Perhaps a slight digression is in order, so I will jot down another event related to the observations already described. It may not have a direct connection with the photographs, yet it seems worth mentioning. I am talking about our cats Boris and Grieta, whom we always take with us to the countryside. In the first days after our arrival, they behaved as usual – stepped daintily through the dew-covered grass, snatched at bugs, brought home mice, but then something suddenly changed. Boris scrambled up a tree, could not make it down and then seemed to be overcome by inexplicable fear. And Grieta seemed telepathically to somehow catch that same fear. It seemed that after Boris had looked at our house and the encircling forest from another angle, both animals began to perceive something more in their surroundings. They began to live as though in a different world – and I don't mean just their ability to hear a mouse rustling near the dustbin, a butterfly hitting the window-pane or a little bird, softly slapping together its wings before taking off from a branch. The fact that cats can see and hear much more than we humans is nothing new – after all, they're only partially domesticated predators.

Observing the suspicion and caution with which they now looked from inside out, I entertained myself with a theory. Perhaps someone else had come up with something similar before me, but it wasn't originality I was after.

We imagine that time is moving forward while space, the surrounding world, stays still, always within reach, available like a painting that has been seen a million times on a museum wall. In a sense this picture is very much like the arrangement of the world as people imagined it in the sixteenth century, namely, that Earth is the centre of every-thing, and other heavenly bodies circle around it. Then came the realisation that the sun is at the centre – every-one has learnt it in history lessons. Yet we entertain a hope that in this hodgepodge of heavenly bodies, atoms and mol-ecules there are some points that remain immutable and we can return to them. Even if the only point in question is ourselves.

We're secure in our belief that we live in a world where we can expect to wake up in the same bed and room we went to sleep in (all right, there are some exceptions, but never mind), where the door will open on to the same street, row of shops or field, where trees will be where they've always been, where the people we encountered yesterday will remain the same the day after tomorrow, and everything else will remain more or less unchanged, irrespective of the hour, day or our regular cycle of falling asleep and waking up.

I must say that this is a rather frivolous view of the world. Boris and Grieta always begin their day outside the house as if someone had changed everything during the night: as if every leaf of grass, every tree, outside table or rock had become something else overnight. Or, as if under the cover of darkness and their own sleep, the house had impercept-ibly moved to another, previously unknown spot. Perhaps it is their wild nature that allows them to see more and to take a more cynical look at the world, without human sentimen-tality. They may be the ones to remind us that by keeping some elements of the past – say, objects or pictures of dead relatives, picture albums or souvenirs from our travels – we are preserving not the lost people or places we once visited, but the non-existence of these people, an unfillable void, a feeling of irreversible loss and the suspicion that we are not there, not in that time to which we would have wanted to return. Even if everything there were completely different than we remember.

Photograph 1

Even though it was already dusk and the air was swarming with mosquitoes when we arrived in the countryside, we went to find the place where the first picture was taken that same evening. There was no wind and, with a fearful whisper only the leaves of aspens were flickering. In the distance, a bird was whistling a monotonous and seemingly sad tune – it couldn't even be called a song as it was a single note sounded repeatedly at a consistent rhythm.

"It means rain," someone said knowingly.

With a sudden fluttering noise, another bird flew up – some kind of owl or hawk – and, with stately flaps of its wings, glided into the depths of the forest.

"It was definitely a different bird, not that one."

"No, of course not."

When we walked out of the forest, we were momentarily blinded by the last rays of the setting sun. They streamed over the roadside brush, over the ends of the bent-grass in the meadow, and the entire world was either black or gleaming gold. And then we were back in the shadows, back to the mosquitoes – along the fence of the cemetery, along the overgrown road, towards where the narrow-gauge used to be.

At the time when the Ventspils-Kolka highway had yet to be built, it was this road, meandering alongside the rails and, at times, crossing it, that locals and their carts used to move from village to village. For instance, to get to the nearby, now abandoned house, people had to turn and cross the railroad, whereas at the neighbouring house, the road had crossed over to the other side of the rails.

The place you can see our house from, along the power line clearing, is dark and bleak. The forest there is overgrown and damp; the ground is covered with shiny black, rotting leaves and lush, dark green vegetation. It looks like there are no new trees or bushes at all: the bark on all of them is cracked and peeling, the trunks are punctuated with bug holes and worried by fungi of various sizes. The trees that have lost their power of resistance are slowly dying, collapsing. One of them has fallen across the old, grass-covered road. Spiders are spinning their webs between the tree trunks, and from the dark waters strewn with small leaves, new swarms of mosquitoes are spawned all summer long. It seems that the sun's rays never penetrate this spot.

Searching for the place from which the photograph was taken, we had to break through thickets of nettles and brambles, and find a way to circumvent a dull, greyish body of water from which crumbling, lifeless trunks emerged like the masts of sunken ships.

Yet even when we reached the appropriate distance, we failed to find the photographer's angle. The explanation of course might be the focal distance of the lens used and thus the angle of vision, yet something was truly perplexing about it all.

It seems that we did find the place where the unknown photographer might have stood. If anyone could stand there at all, the view of the house would probably be identical to the one seen in the picture. But it was impossible to stand there due to the presence of three hefty alders, tightly pressed against one another.

Photograph 2

Finding the angle from which this picture was taken was not at all difficult. It was taken from the middle of our yard, the only difference being that, in contrast to what the picture shows, the outer wall of our shed is not covered with countless shoes. We guessed that it may have been an earlier shed than the one we have now, yet it was a silly thought: the ancestor of our shed would have stood here many decades ago, long before we found this place and first saw it – and long before the invention of digital cameras.

Dzintars, the carpenter who came from Ventspils to build our terrace, suggested that the shoes might have something to do with the notorious leg-cutters of Kurzeme.

"No doubt that this ain't the first or last house with such shoes dryin'," he said in his brusque dialect.

According to a legend popular in these parts, the locals would regularly turn off the lights in the lighthouse and then walk a limping cow with a lantern attached to it. Sailors took it for a lighthouse, went off course and ran on to sandbars, where the locals would then rob the ships of anything they could use – including the boots from the drowned sailors. Since these were hard to pull off swollen legs, they were cut off with the legs inside and then hung to dry in the wind, so that the shrunken limbs would fall out on their own.

Photograph 3

To find the location where this photograph was taken was the most difficult task. Frankly, we failed. We spent several days investigating all forest roads in our four-by-four both on the side of the sea and the narrow strip between the highway and the river, as well as the vast bogs and forests on the opposite bank of the river. Looking for a building we'd never seen before, we even went along the roads, which we wouldn't dare enter if, for instance, we were going to pick mushrooms.

We had to overcome many difficulties and obstacles. A huge birch tree blocked our way and it was impossible to turn around. Using the small axe we keep in the car, we had to cut the trunk in two places – only then could we drag the tree off the road. It would be pointless to describe the several times we got stuck in the loose sand of the former Soviet tank routes. We decided that we should abandon our search when we realised that the car was surrounded by water with sparse, beaver-damaged trees growing in it and the road appeared to have come to an end.

Photograph 4

The oak growing in our yard is exactly the same as in this picture – even the same branches are dead, and that suggests that the picture was taken quite recently. However, there are no ruins around our oak, and there's no evidence that any construction has ever existed side by side with it. And this is not the only peculiarity. For this photograph, too, it was impossible to find the angle from which it was taken. Unless it's some technical trick, the unknown photographer must have been standing in the exact spot where a lime tree has stood for several decades.

Photograph 5

The solution to this one fell into our hands just as easily as we sometimes find the best places for chanterelles, ceps or orange-cap boletuses. In fact, it did happen while we were mushroom picking – one of those times when we didn't feel like journeying to any faraway forests and decided to just do our foraging near the house. We entered the forest through the back gate: that's the gate that doesn't see daily use on the other side of the meadow, and it leads to the road that goes parallel to the former narrow-gauge embankment and the Kolka highway. Frankly, I only remember the gate being driven through on two occasions. The first time was during the renovation of the house in the beginning of the 1990s, when a concrete-mixer lorry came through it and then got stuck between the ponds. The engine couldn't be switched off because the mixer must keep constantly turning, otherwise the concrete would begin to harden, and so the truck kept sinking deeper to the rhythm of the humming engine.

The second time it was a cesspoolage truck that came through the gate. And it too got stuck.

Water from the tank of the truck for cleaning cesspools had to be pumped into the ponds. The concrete truck was pulled out by the Soviet Army – at the time, it was still stationed in Latvia. A tank came from the military base, and the problem was solved in no time. It was a different matter with the other truck. In the immediate vicinity, the only person who still had a tractor was the Liv king who lived in the village. He was tough, obstinate and proud – a man worthy of his ancestors. Recently he'd been sued for illegitimately clearing a path in the dunes to have a shortcut to the sea for his fishing needs. After a long wrangle, he finally trundled over in his old Belarusian tractor, helped pull out the truck and refused any reward.

So we went to the forest on this historic road, turning right, towards the neighbours' house. We noticed the hole in the ground after about twenty metres, on the right side, about three metres from the road. It looked even more overgrown than in the picture, yet it was clear that it was the same spot. And certainly it was the same bunker in which the former owner of the house – the father of the forester we met – used to sleep off his "teeter-totters", whatever they were.

The bunker was a small but substantial construction. A fringe of damp moss hung from the small opening; a large, round spider's web blocked the entrance, yet the brick walls, albeit covered in dark green moss and mould, were solid, without a single crack. It may be that all this talk about the teeter-totters was just some rumour spread by locals, and the man had simply given in to fear of a nuclear war, which was common in Soviet times. Even at primary school we were taught what "everyone must learn and know" – namely various plans of action in case the "enemy" decided to drop an atom bomb somewhere nearby. One of the most important elements in this planning was building a safe underground shelter.

The floor of the bunker was sandy and dry; a few rocks and sticks, as well as a burnt piece of plank were the only litter. Yet in the middle of it all, there was something else: a large motionless animal with thick, grey fur that must have chosen this as its last shelter.

While we were busy around the entrance to the bunker, a bright red Audi with black doors passed us at a slow, watchful speed. It was impossible to discern the faces of those sitting inside, yet we did feel their glances.

Photograph 6

It was a sunny afternoon when we went to the so-called Doctor's House. Several years ago, we had started a utopian project: we'd hoped to clear the brush and develop a new and straighter path to the sea. Up to where the narrow-gauge railway had been, everything went reasonably smoothly. A small bridge had to be built over a hollow, some fallen trees cleared away, a path cut through the brambles and a plank thrown across a marsh. Further on, over the narrow-gauge track, our path led directly into the yard of the Doctor's House – the driveway at the time was not overgrown and torn up by wild boar. A short time ago, it had been driven on rather frequently – probably someone was taking away the boards and logs of the torn-down shed. Black and red currant bushes were concealed amongst the tall grass, peonies bloomed amongst the bent-grass leaves, and on the edge of the forest, protected by impenetrable wild raspberry bushes, grew some gnarled, moss-covered apple trees. Further on, work on the path did not go as smoothly as before. Right behind the Doctor's House, there was a deep ditch full of stagnant, stinking water, and then we would have had to force our way through the forest. No wonder we abandoned the idea a short while after, and the path we had put in place soon grew over and disappeared into the scrub.

We did know it, yet what we saw surprised us neverthe-less. The doctor's road was so overgrown that only someone who knew of its existence could notice it amongst the rest of the bushes growing by the narrow-gauge tracks. Where once the contour of a yard delineated by a garden and berry bushes could still be discerned, now was a wild meadow overgrown with bushes and brambles. The Doctor's House was where it always had been, and I probably already ment-ioned that it was not even a real house. Of the house itself, only the ruins of the big chimney remained, and the last resident of this house had lived in a kind of a garden house with one room and a single window. The door to it was wide open, and people, different animals, and the seasons had had their way with it. The honeysuckle was coiling into the house through the broken window.

Having torn through the bramble jungle, we stepped back and tried to locate the place the picture was taken from. Yet, no matter where we stood, it seemed all the time that we were too close to the house; the picture showed the slant of its roof was much more gently sloping in the perspective. On the hill behind the long since burnt-down house were two substantial oaks. Only standing right next to them, the view of the house was approximately the way it was in the picture. Almost the same, yet slightly different. It was a difference of only a few dozen centimetres, but it was enough. As if the photographer had stood right where one of the oaks grew now.

Photograph 7

We went to the cemetery at approximately the same hour of the day when the picture must have been taken. The setting sun stretched the long shadows of roadside bushes over the meadow that hadn't been mown that year. Even though the cemetery is nearby, we rarely go there. We're not locals and no relative of ours has been buried there. At the times when we have gone there, we've entertained ourselves by trying to locate the last names of villagers of our acquaintance and figure out the relationships between the living and the dead. Cemeteries are places that reveal who amongst the core population of this Liv township belongs to the largest and most influential families who have lived here for generations, who has been passing through and which families have, for some reason, petered out or moved elsewhere. Here everybody is close together, unlike the township itself, which has scattered itself through the nearby forests, meadows and scrublands.

We wandered around the cemetery for over an hour; the sun had long since set, the sky swiftly darkened and finally we had to give up without finding the gravesite we were looking for. Finding the right angle, however, presented no difficulty. It seemed that the picture was taken from right behind the large travertine monument built for probably the most well known of the local families. Yet there were no more graves over there: a few metres away was the bright green chicken-wire fence put up not long ago, and right where the grave was seen in the picture grew a large fir that had to be several decades old.

Video 1

We had no hope of finding out the location where the short video clip was shot. It simply contained too little information. Coming home from the cemetery we wondered if the video might have been shot right there on the road leading to our house in similar light to what we had that evening. In daytime, our house can be seen briefly from this spot at the end of the road. Now the reflection of the light from the table lamp in the kitchen window flashed far ahead, immediately disappearing behind the trees. We had with us a head torch. I turned it off and now, in the darkness, we took a couple of steps back and then forward.

Darkness, lamp in the window, darkness again. The large and never to be seen bird once again took to wing with a noise resembling a deep sigh, and soundlessly flew into the deep woods. The Milky Way was crossing the sky right above our heads, shining brightly.

[drawing]

There was no direct connection with the camera we'd found, but not long after that, we decided to set up a motion-activated night-vision camera for a few nights. During the summer and now, as autumn was drawing near, various animals were busy near the house and even in the yard. Wild boar tore up not only the meadow but, from time to time, even the yard. At the end of the pond, a beaver had begun its activities – he'd already gnawed off several big trees and, in his gnawing frenzy, even attacked one of the rowans. In the middle of the pond was something that could be considered the foundation of his winter house and, at one end, he'd dug a substantial canal, lowering the level of the water by half a metre. In addition, he'd destroyed part of the spruce hedge that separated the pond and the forest from our yard. Unconsciously and with an indifferent diligence, the beaver was destroying the borders between the wilderness and home, like some messenger of entropy, reminding us about the true order of this forest landscape created in the Ice Age. From generation to generation, man could mow, cut, remove tree stumps, burn, tend to and renew, yet it only took a brief moment of inattention for new shoots and forest creatures to appear in and take over meadows, fields and yards.

A moose had wandered into our yard during our absence. The evidence was a large pile of excrement and its sleeping place – for some unknown reason, it had decided to lie down in the spiraea bush, which was now completely destroyed. In the distance, elk were bellowing nonstop – one day, we saw about half a dozen run across the road – and only rarely would a shot interrupt the noise. It was an unequal battle because people were now a minority and, just like in the *Green Tale*, which I read as a child, the forest, with all its trees, bushes, beasts and birds, was taking over the city, breaking into our homes there. And it had settled into our home for quite some time in the form of a bird's nest collection on a shelf, various plants brought from all around and framed on the wall or pressed between the pages of books, and deer and elk antlers found in the forest. In our absence it tried to enter as different rodents or bugs. Spiders were busy making webs not only across our outdoor paths, but also in the corners or rooms, on windowpanes and door frames. Each time we arrived in the country, we tore them, wiped them off or sucked them up in the vacuum cleaner, but they were replaced by others shortly thereafter.

Every year with the coming of autumn, we felt an increasing restlessness – the "mushroom urge" as we called it – leading us to thoroughly inspect the memorised spots where chanterelles, ceps, orange-cap boletuses and saffron milk caps grew, not to mention "knights", the sought-after baby orange-cap boletuses. With the mushrooms we gathered, we not only brought the forest into our home, but also into ourselves. Even though we were newcomers, we participated in the wild food chain. We could talk about a good or bad mushroom year in the manner of some primitive hunter-gatherer tribe, as if our chances of surviving the winter depended on what we picked in the forest. It wasn't that our survival depended on mushrooms, of course – we had simply become mushroom-addicted. Imperceptibly, they'd taken the upper hand.

This was not a good mushroom year; we even joked that mushrooms might have changed the strategy of their survival and chosen a new tactic. There were very few chanterelles, hardly any ceps, and yet there were scores of gypsy mushrooms, which we have never valued. They grew in circle after circle, as if teasing us as we wandered through the forest with our empty baskets and little knives, grumbling that there were more than enough mushrooms, but none of them were any good.

We tried to find all kinds of explanations for the poor mushroom crop. Maybe, as a result of rebuilding the big road, the ground water level had changed, we reasoned. Circles of gypsy mushrooms may have been growing where the underground water mains intersected. Or maybe they delineated some geological anomalies, cracks in underground rocks or power points perceptible only with some highly developed sense organs. Knowing that what we see above ground is only the reproductive parts of mushrooms, and the true mushrooms are mycelium spread under the moss and soil, we let our imaginations run wild as we sat in the kitchen baking apples and drinking wine, and developed a theory that the mycelium could be connected to the collective mind or consciousness of the forest. After all, there is talk of the symbiosis or peculiar cooperation between mushrooms and trees, as one life form supports the existence of another. Or could it be that the mycelium itself is this invisible nerve network of the forest, and not only the forest, but nature as such – something very much like our Internet?

Mushrooms, fungi, live everywhere – starting with our homes and even our bodies, and ending with forests and meadows. Thus it would be no surprise if, for instance, the army of edible mushrooms decided to move to safer spots not yet discovered by mushroom pickers, leaving in their stead those that are usually of no interest to us. Furthermore, who says that the other plants and animals in the forest could not act in communication with the mushrooms? Just think of it: trees whose roots are intertwined with the mycelium, beavers gnawing at the trees, elk and moose who eat mushrooms, the fungi of mould and yeast that consume what remains of dead trees and animals…

We humans behave in this world like aggressively inclined arrivals from some other planet, armed for militant self-preservation. We constantly "fight against entropy": we mow and weed everything; we level out molehills; we clean and disinfect, and saturate with antiseptics.

One time we were amused by the maps drawn in *Kurzeme*, authored by Sigurds Rusmanis and Ivars Vīks: on these maps, straight lines connected various places in the vicinity of our country home, forming precise geometric figures. These, the authors claimed, once were the sacred places of our ancestors. It was difficult to imagine how our ancestors, dwelling tens and hundreds of kilometres from each other, managed to place their sanctums with such precision. It seemed that the thought of setting up a sacred place here or there must have been prompted by some greater reason, regardless of what one might call it: God, gods, forces of nature, ancestral spirits, or perhaps some consciousness uniting all living beings and even inanimate objects – something like the noosphere, the shared consciousness of the earth described by the French Jesuit theologian Pierre Teilhard de Chardin. Our fantasies carried us late into the night and, as the fire was going out, we noticed that the figures connecting the ancestral holy sites resembled a drawing on the wall of our kitchen. Some years ago, the coal drawing was made by our friend E who, at the time, was studying theoretical physics. On a summer evening we'd talked him into explaining the Big Bang theory and the latest views of physicists on the expansion (or contraction) of the universe, as well as the relationship between space and time.

[drawing]

We borrowed the night-vision camera from a well-known birdwatcher, attached it to the rowan in front of the house and went to sleep. Yet sleep escaped us. Acorns rattled and rolled over the roof; the marten, a long-time resident in our house, rustled within the walls; wood-borers worked the floorboards and beams; a cricket chirped behind the fireplace; a doomed winter fly, agitated by the heat of the stove, zigzagged chaotically through the room; the wind sighed in the old birch, and the entire environs of the house seemed to be full of wide-open nostrils, alert eyes and strained ears. Without being able to see anything ourselves, we'd become the centre of attention.

That night, I remembered my childhood toy bear Mika. It is amazing that one of the most popular toys throughout the world and for centuries should be the effigy of a very dangerous and predatory wild animal. Mika was only a few months younger than me – he was given to me on my first New Year's Eve and since then we have been practically inseparable. Even later, after I had graduated from school, Mika moved with me to every flat I lived in, got to meet my friends and was always somewhere close by. And even when he wasn't, the idea of Mika, if we can call it that, was always present. It began when I was very young: going somewhere with my parents and looking out the window of a bus or train, I would point to "Mika's houses", "Mika's gardens", or note some other object connected with Mika's life. These might be separated by dozens of kilometres – it made no difference. In Mika's biography, these distances vanished and he lived in a compact and clearly delineated world which could easily be accommodated by a single drawing pad.

I suddenly remembered Mika when I realised that I had no idea where he now was. I tried to recall when I'd last seen my bear and realised that it was quite a long time ago. Was it not the time that I began to worry about moths damaging him? Mika had already suffered enough. I hadn't even got to school when he was so threadbare that my mother, for appearance's sake, knitted him a little striped wool vest with blue buttons. She had knitted one for me too, so this helped me even more to identify with Mika and him with me. The foam stuffing hardened and became fragile, eventually crumbling to dust, so Mika's body looked like the wizened flesh of an old man. And now I could not for the life of me remember where and when I had seen Mika last.

Renouncing the possibility of sleep, I went downstairs to the kitchen. The feeling that someone was watching me from the dark outside became even stronger. In the black panes of the windows I only saw the reflection of the brightly lit kitchen and myself and it was clear that a man, animal or something else – but what? – could come very close to the house, stare at me and remain invisible. At that very moment, the camera flashed, I started and perhaps even muttered some expletive. But then I felt ashamed and rebuked myself for my stupid reaction. After all, I had put the camera there myself, so why would I be spooked by it? In the brief flash of the light, I could not see anything because I had turned away from the window. I sat at the kitchen window for half an hour, looking into the darkness, but nothing more happened.

Once again I had thought about what we would do and how we would react if some robbers or, say, escaped convicts, broke into our house. How could we resist them? What would be our chances of escaping? Probably it would be simpler to do it from the second floor, as the only way to get there would be by taking the stairs or climbing up on to the balcony. Yet upstairs there is almost nothing that could be used as a weapon. Except the poker, dustpan and firewood basket. I am not easily frightened, but I took an axe upstairs.

We woke up late and immediately went to see if we had managed to take a picture of something. My suspicion that someone was in the yard turned out to be well grounded. The lawn in front of the house looked as if it had been ploughed. Wild boar or perhaps some other animal had shown admirable diligence and care in peeling back a large swathe of the turf. The night had kept the beaver busy, for he had chewed off several bushes and pulled them into the water. As if mocking our dismay, several jays were romping through the oak screeching wildly and dropping clusters of leaves at our feet.

When we plugged the camera into the computer, we were disappointed. The memory card did not contain many dozens of portraits of night creatures – there was only one, apparently the one taken when I happened to be in the kitchen. The camera had flashed with a delay of a few seconds, so the light had only caught the hind quarters and tail of the animal. It was our good old mink that sometimes crossed the yard at this spot even in the light of day. It favoured this route so much that there was already a well-defined path in the grass. In other words, the picture did not turn out and I was about to close it when I noticed something else. In the dark brushwood on the other side of the fence, a rather sizeable figure was seen. The silhouette was blurry, yet the figure was so large that it could only be a person or an elk or a moose facing us.

In order to get to the place where the mysterious figure was seen, you had to cut through a thicket of brambles and cross a gully overgrown with ferns. After that there was a small, almost treeless hill. In Soviet times, resin was extracted from some of the firs – the trunks still showed scars in the herring-bone shape, cut with a special tool and now overgrown with moss. Many of the dead trees were without any branches: storms had broken their tops and only black, rotted stalks were left standing. One of them solved the mystery of the figure seen in the photograph – at the place where supposedly some creature had stood once, a healthy alder had grown. Now it was dead and almost collapsed on to itself. Only a trunk of my height still stood with all the bark missing.

Even though I had heard of rotten wood glowing in the

dark, I'd never seen it with my own eyes. We decided to go out at night to see if the dead trunk really glowed. But then I somehow leaned against it, there was a loud crack and it collapsed, falling apart in many bug-perforated pieces. Even if the figure had been this old alder stub, it could no longer be seen from the house, rendering any night-time observations impossible. Yet I did pick up some of the dead pieces wood and propped them against the fence in the yard. After all, if the entire trunk glowed, then its parts should do likewise, I thought.

The day passed without us doing anything important and just biding time, waiting for the evening. For a while I sat by the pond, hoping to see the beaver again. Once it swam out of the channel it had dug, looking straight at me without the slightest trace of shame, then moved to the opposite bank and, still keeping an eye on me, began to chew on some osier shoots. But now there was no sign of the beaver, though some frogs splashed around in the shallow part and tiny fish were flashing about near the surface. Sitting like that by the pond, I suddenly caught some movement out of the corner of my eye – it seemed as if a person was walking there, slowly. Yet when I turned my head, no one was there. Such visual or auditory tricks are common here. On many occasions, as I've sat alone in the kitchen or veranda, I've had the feeling that someone was crossing the yard or passing the window. On the second floor, it sometimes seems as if someone is talking or moving about on the first. But of course there's no one to be seen.

Even though I liked to think of these phenomena as ghosts, I knew well enough that nothing like that exists, that these are simply phantoms created by my oversensitive imagination. Only in this middle-of-the-forest silence, where only the sounds of nature reign, one's vision and hearing free themselves of the pollution created by the chaos and noise of the city and begin to perceive even supposedly inaudible sounds and invisible movement. It was the same with the light pollution in the city, where it was impossible to see not only the clusters of faraway galaxies but even the brightest of stars. I remember that at the very beginning, I was always surprised it was possible to hear the sound of the waves here, in the middle of the forest, and some time passed before I realised that the monotonous din of engines, brought over by the wind, came from the big ships gliding on the horizon.

In the evening, we again set up the camera and, when it was dark, went out on to the porch to take a look at the pieces of tree trunk propped up against the fence. The sky was clear and I saw a bright dot glide between the stars – it must have been a plane or a satellite. I stood there motion-less for quite a while. The edge of the forest looked black from the dark and the dead pieces of wood did not glow. As I turned to go back in, the flash worked with an almost inaudible click.

IV. JOURNAL

Undated

I understood that, during my travels, my home, my dear estate and my homeland were no longer concrete places, but distant figments of my imagination. They did not have anything in common with everyday reality, with places where I found myself physically, and it could be said that reality followed me everywhere like a shell, limited in space, and that beyond those limits reigned memories, fanciful notions, fantasies and conjectures. Just like a passenger on a train, who mostly sees what takes place inside the carriage as the outside world flashes past, I sped through the war and those chaotic times, mostly concerned about what I needed for my survival, here and now; it was impossible to closely examine and remember the world outside my immediate situation, and many things remained hidden. If I sometimes thought of my mother and father or the estate, I realised that I could not even recall my parents' faces. Even my favourite places formed an abstract whole in my thoughts, and I dearly missed all the scents, colours, tastes and other sensations which once were so important to me.

During my absence, I didn't think much about it, and this realisation hit me only now when I returned to the estate and found my mother and father alive and well, albeit having aged in a disturbingly short time. The arrival of the Germans had caused them worry and more than one fearful moment.

One night, a group of them had made their way to the estate – my parents woke up to muffled noises in the veranda and German voices. Afraid to move, Mother and

Father lay awake until dawn. Only in full daylight did Father gather the courage to go and take a look. The veranda door was open, an axe was lying on the floor and a box with tulip bulbs was missing from the table. "In the dark, it probably looked like food," Mother guessed. Another time, the Germans had even come into the guest room. They'd turned on the light and my parents heard the clatter of china. In the morning there was cigarette smoke in the air and four crystal shot glasses had been taken out of the sideboard and left on the table.

It is difficult to explain but, when I came to Vidzeme by train a few days ago, I saw the difference immediately. The trees, forests, bushes, meadows and fields seemingly were the same as in Russia, yet there was something that made me see this landscape with different eyes. What was it that made this country – if not special, then different? Was it just my own perception, or was there some objective truth to it?

I thought about this today as I lay there in the tall grass, looking up into the forked branches of the old lime tree. I could have lain like this in the prince's park on his estate near Moscow – there too, blades of grass would rustle, branches would sway in the wind, and yet the feeling would be entirely different. And suddenly it seemed to me that I had guessed the answer.

There, at Fyodor Pavlovich's place, the wastes of Russia would be stretching all around me and I would be a tiny midge of no concern to anyone. War, revolution – even such storms simply came and went there, without being able to change much of anything. It was the distinct scale, more familiar to me, which made everything different and so special here. I had walked from Riga to Valka in fewer than five days. Within a week, I could make it from Riga to the most remote parts of Latgale or a seaside village in Kurzeme. It would only take a few weeks to get from one Latvian-inhabited place to any other. In a horse-drawn carriage, by train or car it would be child's play. And wherever I went, I would run into someone I knew. There are so few of us, we are close to each other and our land is small. As you cross the border, leaving Russia, the world seems to contract: hills and valleys, forests and riverbeds come closer; everything is plain to see yet changing constantly. Everything is as restless and changing as our history, which is primarily filled with strangers fighting over this small and seemingly insignificant piece of land.

[drawing]

Is there any point in having our own state? But then one could ask if there is any point to my own existence. As far as I know, no great philosopher has been able to find an answer to this question that would satisfy everyone. Where do I come from, who am I and where am I going – these, or close to these, were the questions posed by Kant. Yet the great Konigsberg philosopher also understood that out of the "crooked wood of humanity" nothing straight could be fashioned. Anything we touch comes out wrong: the good, which we desire, we do not do and the bad, which we deplore, we do.

So who am I and why do I exist? I would think that the old cultured nations of Europe – the Greeks or even the Germans – do not ask these questions very often. It's not that they know the answers. Yet we Latvians – and I am absolutely sure of this – would want to puzzle over our distinctiveness and our *raison d'être* even if we someday managed to get free and establish our own state, and had held it for, say, a century.

Even if that came to pass, we would somehow feel undeserving of our freedom, always insecure and not at all sure that this freedom wouldn't be taken from us at any moment. We would continue to behave like Adam and Eve after they were thrown out of Paradise where they had been completely safe, when they had to decide their own future, make a living and secure themselves against danger.

This may be the reason why the constant and increasing aspirations towards independence are accompanied by a greater resistance to freedom. It is the feeling that one should always look before one leaps because the whole wide world is full of threats and danger.

The old European nations are quite the opposite – they live like illusion-driven simpletons who think that any blow fate inflicts includes an advantageous or lucky break designed to favour them. I think it was Lev Tolstoy who once wrote that any individual person feels crushed upon discovering in his own experience that the general rules of nature do in fact apply. A Latvian, as opposed to Tolstoy's protagonist – it may have been Ivan Ilyich – feels crushed even before any such discovery, and therefore decides that it's best not to do anything.

We humans have never been satisfied with what we already have. The above-mentioned Adam and Eve are a case in point. We begin to use tools, we invent the wheel, we discover new lands and heavenly bodies, yet we do so only to feel satiated, better than any other creature, and safe. And this is the reason why the entire human race and other living beings are mostly destined to suffer. Not just individual people and animals, but often whole countries and nations. And it is most pronounced with us, Latvians. We are so accustomed to having nothing – no property, no freedom, and even no language of our own for a long period – and that's why we live like starving animals, always ravenous, always suspicious both of strangers and our own people.

1 October
Our lives are spent in an endless attempt to live like a human and to learn what that is. And yet, as a wise man once wrote, even if a young man every day learnt by heart

a hundred pages about how one should live, he must remember that several dozen million unread pages will remain in that book. While you are reading and trying to learn how to live and how to be human, it can turn out that life has already ended. All of us – Tidriķis, Alberts and I – came to the conclusion during our meeting that there is no reason to hope for any improvement, and everything is moving towards a decline. Perhaps we have not gone to fancy enough schools or been endowed with great minds, yet many wise men, particularly Schopenhauer and Nietzsche, reached the same conclusions. And yet people are prey to a conviction bordering on obsession that only progress or a relentless striving to invent something new will bring long-awaited improvements in all areas. This war proves that this is not the case.

Upon my return to the estate, I discovered that Father had lost a finger during my time away. Luckily, it was the small finger of his left hand, but he was quite emotional about it because he now considered himself a cripple. Despite his age, he still did all the most important outside chores himself and in the spring had decided to saw off some dry ash branches in the park. One of them fell and pressed his hand to the trunk. The doctor was called and he concluded that the finger could not be saved and would have to be amputated. This is how, very prosaically, a simple tree or nature can settle scores with a man, the same man who thinks that he has long since risen above nature and is unconnected to it.

Another event was my mother's story of grief about her beloved cat. In the middle of winter he disappeared, no longer came to get warm in the house or in the barn with the cow. Foxes were immediately the main suspects, as they had been seen in great numbers near the estate and sometimes would impudently slink around the barn, scouting the place in hope of grabbing one of Mother's old chickens. Only in the spring did Father find the cat: in all likelihood, he'd left the house to die a natural death. He'd crawled on to a fence post at the edge of the meadow and remained there under the cover of snow all winter. We, the people, had in the end turned out to be strangers to him. Nature called the cat to itself and he had loyally answered it.

4 October

It seemed that Father wanted to say something but changed his mind. As I was leaving, he walked me to the door, seemed to begin saying something, but stopped himself mid-phrase. I tried to get out of him what he wanted to say, but all in vain, he just waved dismissively. Mother stood by the window and waved when I looked back.

By train, in which most of the passengers were German soldiers, I got to Usma. The plan was that before continuing on to Ventspils and later maybe to Liepāja, I could spend a few days with the local forester Mačs Lielmežs, who turned out to be our relative on my mother's side – her father's cousin or something. I once again had a chance to note that our land is so small and there are so few of us that anywhere it is possible to run into some relative or at least an acquaintance. These two days with Mačs reinforced my conviction that freedom should not be sought in people or political regimes but in our own natural roots.

"My freedom is right here," Mačs said when I asked for his opinion on founding an independent state. He too thought that it was not the country farmsteads, roads, city buildings and institutions but our forests, brushwood, oaks, rivers and lakes that either allow or do not allow us to be free.

"God is no baby," Mačs said, smoking his pipe. It seemed that he had become at one with the forest and all of nature.

"Just think how few of us are alive here compared to those who have died in all these hundreds and thousands of years," he mused. "And they have all been buried in the ground – that same ground we plough and in which trees and everything else put down their roots. Of course, you can try to attach some religious meaning to it all, but I'm not religious. But I recognise that we have a much closer connection with our predecessors than most would like to think. To me, it is exactly this that represents the life after death that so many faiths talk about."

As confirmation of what Mačs was saying, the lady of the house put all kinds of gifts of nature on the table. There were venison hors d'oeuvres as well as an eel caught right there in the lake, sautéed sauerkraut, lynx meatballs and cloudberry mousse.

"We want for nothing here," Mačs said. "The forest, lake and field bring us everything we need. Both the edible and inedible. If you are able to take care of everything and there is enough of everything, then you need no overlords and no government. The only ones who need governing are those incapable of taking care of themselves and making their own decisions – those who are ill or crippled, lazy or otherwise deficient."

What Mačs was saying reminded me of what I had read some time ago about an American who had left his life in the city, built a primitive hut on the shore of a lake and lived in it for several years in complete solitude, thus demonstrating that it is possible to live without all the achievements of technology and civilisation, without the expensive arrangements modern man is so accustomed to. His goal was to show that seeking material wealth inevitably makes a person live in material or spiritual indebtedness, a slave to oneself, while any student would be able to build himself a cheap dwelling that he could use for the rest of his life.

I had walked to Mačs's house quite a distance around the lake, but to get back to the highway he took me in his boat. It must be because of my childhood in the estate by Lake Ķīšezers that any body of water is particularly close to my heart, and this boat ride gave me much pleasure and even stirred my soul. First, as we had reached the open water, finding ourselves in the middle of the calm expanse, I had the fleeting sensation that we were at the very centre of the world. But then we were already at the opposite shore and, through a barely noticeable opening in the reeds, glided into a narrow, meandering creek. Here, the forest and the bog came right up to the water on both sides, and Mačs pointed out the paths beaten by animals as they came to drink. Our arrival disturbed a few big birds, but we did not see any other animals. And then, to my great surprise, the creek once again guided us back to a lake. This was no longer the big lake, but much smaller, and as it turned out the highway was on its shore. I said my goodbyes to Mačs and expressed my gratitude. I noticed that two of the fingers of his right hand were stiff, crooked and motionless like the branches of a tree. Although I am hardly superstitious, I decided that it was a good sign. I'd be hard put to explain it, yet it seems that this meeting reinforced some conviction and resolve in me.

6 October

Up to now, my "journalist's" journey through Vidzeme and the newly established Baltic Duchy had been free of big mishaps and danger (in the beginning, I even sent correspondences to the editorial address in Moscow from Pskov, Riga and Tukums), but near Dundaga, my exploits almost came to an end.

I had decided to explore the narrow-gauge railways and bridges built by the Germans, but I was thwarted by the false sense of security I had developed in Riga. Although many of city's residents had left, Riga was still a metropolis housing all kinds of people.

Riga was under the Germans, yet a great variety of meetings held by people deciding on and dreaming about Latvia's future continued to be convened in the city by Bolshevik supporters and other demagogues stirring up trouble and motivated either by a primitive impulse for personal gain or the interests of the remaining great powers. Because of this chaos, where many had something to hide and equally many were interested in finding out those secrets and casting light on them, it was much easier to remain unnoticed than in the country, where there were very few people known to the authorities locally.

Realising that no secrecy would be possible there – even if I changed my appearance as I had done in Riga – I decided to put my cards on the table, so to speak.

So first I went to the commandant's office to announce myself, for I reckoned that bold actions would serve best to dissipate any suspicion regarding my person. I was taken to an officer by the name of either von Seichler or von Zeichler. He was a youngish man – even younger than I was, I think – and compared to the Kaiser's portrait that was hanging next to him on the wall, he almost looked liked a child dressed up in a carefully pressed uniform. I introduced myself, showing my documents and the letters from the newspaper *Раннее утро* appointing me its special correspondent in the Duchy of Courland.

At that moment I had no idea that the Bolsheviks had already closed the paper in the summer, deeming it harmful to the Soviet power. The Germans also had no idea about this, but my showing up seemed to them too flamboyant to be unsuspicious.

I had walked through the palace gate a free man, but in a split second everything turned very unpleasant. The young officer who, as far as I could see, was giving orders there, seemed amused, called over two soldiers and had them take me away "until the situation is clarified". I was not treated as an enemy or even roughly, yet I knew full well that in such cases the slightest slip-up could prove fatal. For the moment, it didn't feel like I was a prisoner, as I wasn't locked up but merely taken to a small corner room at the end of the first-floor hallway. It appeared that they didn't see me as anyone important, and I was allowed to keep all my things. The door was not locked, but I knew that one of the soldiers had stayed behind to guard me. The room had a narrow, barred window, through which I could see some bare trees and a pond. There was a simple chair and a wobbly table on the uneven floor. You could turn the chair any which way, but it was impossible to place it so that all four legs had purchase on the ground. That wasn't really necessary, however, as I had no interest in sitting. The room was not heated and freezing cold seeped through the damp stone walls.

I paced my place of imprisonment, trying to hatch different escape plans. Since several hours had passed, evening was approaching and I understood that with every moment that I spent there without doing anything, I reduced my chances of getting out alive. If the Germans were trying to gather some information on me via telegrams to Riga of Valka, I could not give them too much time. Even though it was a cloudy day, I could tell by the light that the sun was about to set, and I decided to act.

I have fought in more than one battle. In order to survive, I have had to commit various acts, even ignominious ones, yet I have never felt any guilt, for this happened in wartime or during revolutionary chaos when only one rule applied – survival of the fittest. This case seemed different. Even though enemy forces were involved, the war was over – at least on paper. And yet, in order to get free, I felt that I had to use rather ignoble methods.

I opened the door a crack and told the guard that all day I had not used the toilet. The guard, a round-faced runt of a man, pointed to the other end of the hallway without any argument. Having walked me to the toilet, he remained outside waiting, and I took care of my business. What happened next took place in just a few moments and so quickly that there was no time to think or remember anything. I have managed to recall it here only because I'd carefully planned my actions whilst walking down the hallway.

Having swung open the toilet door, I slammed the heel of my left hand under the nose of the little soldier, and without letting him recover, I grabbed him by the collar, pulled him forward and kneed him. Falling, he reached for his rifle, but I used his fall to grab him by the throat, turn his back to me and pull him into the toilet. The German was trying to escape my grip, but I held him like a vice, strangling him and banging his head against the stone wall until I could feel no resistance. Although I was winded, I held my breath and listened. Everything was quiet. Having slipped the German's bayonet behind the top of my boot, I stole back to my "cell", threw the sack of my belongings across my shoulder and, deliberately slowly, went to the exit.

As I had suspected, several guards were placed by the gate. Although I was in civilian clothes, I gave them a military salute and, without quickening my pace walked beside the castle's wall and moat towards the train station. Although calm on the outside, my senses were heightened, particularly my hearing, as I had to know if they'd discovered my disappearance.

It happened soon enough. I had reached the windmill when I heard excited voices and profanities. Horses neighed, whips were cracked angrily, horseshoes clattered. I rushed across the footbridge but, as there was still some light, a rider saw me from the end of the road. He stopped his horse, informed his buddies that were lagging behind and a split second later, five or six riders were after me. A few shots rang out. There was no time for counting, so I rushed into the scrubland and rolled down a steep slope into a ravine cut through by a little river – horses would not want to go down there. But it was not over. Orders were shouted and, as I had expected, infantry were called to help. Since I was not armed, they probably thought that there would be no problem catching me. It was now already almost dark, and I could hear twigs cracking behind me as my pursuers slid into the ravine.

I had no intention of running across the ravine. Breaking through the brushwood would have been too slow and noisy, and running along the riverbed didn't seem like a good idea. As soon as I was sure that my pursuers had come into the ravine, I scrambled out of it and, keeping close to the houses and windmill fence, slipped away from the river and the hue and cry I was the sole cause of. The racket was accompanied by the loud barking of the windmill dogs who had got a whiff of my scent, but fortunately no one paid them any attention, for the noise the pursuers were making by the bridge was so great that it could stir up neighbourhoods near and far. Now it was almost completely dark and only in the west was there a narrow strip of light above the horizon.

After I had got away from the houses and run across the mowed pasture, I noticed that my entire left sleeve was wet. That's when I also began to feel pain and realised that one of the bullets had hit me. There was still a fine drizzle and it was now completely dark, but I took off the outer layer of my clothes and saw that the bullet had hit my upper arm; it had torn out a sizeable piece of flesh, but no worse damage had been done. My arm was bleeding heavily, however, so I tried to dress the wound with a piece of cloth I tore from my shirt.

With that done I continued on my way, keeping close to the edge of the road and constantly cocking my ears to hear any suspicious movement, and got to the railroad. I did not dare walk on the rails, for I wasn't sure that they were unguarded; also – someone might have driven on them. The railroad was of great help, however, for otherwise, lacking any maps or landmarks, I might have quickly got lost in my search for a shortcut and met my demise in the swamps of Šlītere.

Though I didn't feel much pain, the blood continued

to flow and that was probably why I began to tire. Having been detained, I hadn't eaten all day and now at night in the middle of forests and swamps there was not much I could hope for or rely on. The time for mushroom and berry picking was past, and if there had been anything edible in the forest, I couldn't have found it in the dark anyway. The only refreshment was a little water I scooped up at the edge of the forest, which tasted of iron. As I walked, I tried to cheer myself up by humming wartime songs – supposing that these tunes can be considered at all cheerful:

> "Will I see my dear, sweet girl,
> Will I still hear my mother's voice…"

I slid down the steep bank of the dune by the Šlītere lighthouse. For a while, the rails of the German narrow-gauge, set in a bridge built of long pine trunks, loomed right above my head, making an arch and disappearing into the forest on the coastal side. It was becoming possible to make things out in the dark in spite of the new moon, because the wind had scattered the rain clouds and the entire sky was full of bright stars. When my eyes adjusted to this dim light, I could clearly make out the shiny rails ahead of me as well as the nearby trees and the jagged forest line.

> "The green coat is pressing on my chest
> Every day like the ruthless night hag [lietuvēns] …"

I heard a sound and stopped humming. Someone or something was noisily approaching me from the left. Fallen trees cracking, fir branches swishing and footsteps could be heard. Startled, I first thought that it might be my pursuers who, incredibly, had caught up with and overtaken me and were now attacking from the flank. Yet soon enough I realised that it could not be people – the footsteps were too fast and they were moving too heavily and confidently through the dark forest. As a precaution I immediately tried to assume a supine position, but slid on the ground that was covered with wet and cold leaves, and landed directly on my wounded arm.

I must have yelled out from the pain and that may have saved me from a stampede – a pack of animals had been running right at me. At the very last minute they changed direction, dashed past me, leapt over the embankment and disappeared into the forest on the other side. With my whole body I felt the shaking of the ground under the weight of the running animals, saw the white steam of their breath and smelt the sharp scent of their sweat. I had never seen such animals in the wild and so close by, but judging by their size, energy and antlers that adorned a head here and there I concluded that they must have been elk. Although my wound hurt, this encounter with at least a dozen strong and free wild animals filled me with a strange energy I had never previously encountered. Sliding down the embankment, I got to my feet and was full of resolve to continue on my way, but right then I was once again startled by movement nearby in the forest. As opposed to the free and noble elk hurtling through the scrubland, who shot through the night and thicket without being afraid to make a noise and, to my eyes, courageously confronting their future, I was now being approached by something stealthy, cautious, cowardly, starving, yet desperate and therefore particularly dangerous.

First one, then another and yet another pair of eyes flashed in the dark. Soon I saw about ten eyes forming a circle around me. Even though I could not make out their owners, it seemed that they were looking at me with their heads bent, scowling. Wolves! A single word darted through my mind. They had been chasing the elk and now their predatory noses had smelt me, my bloody arm and blood-soaked clothes. I had encountered wolves before, but not like this – face-to-face, alone at night. In the war years the wolves had multiplied. During winter battles they were quite a scourge for they managed to sneak up on the fallen and gnaw on their unburied, frozen flesh. It was difficult and time-consuming to dig graves in the frozen ground, so we often had to bury what remained of the wolves' meal. It was also not always possible to chase them away, particularly because the noise of a shot or something else could betray our positions and situation to the enemy.

In many a battle or skirmish, I have observed typical human behaviour when lives are at risk. This behaviour divides people into four different psychological types, and each is characteristic of the animal world. The first type is characterised by freezing up. I am sure that man has inherited this from more primitive beings who hope to survive by hiding, flattening themselves to the ground and pretending to be invisible or dead. It is not hard to imagine that with people and under conditions of war such behaviour is foolish and often proves deadly. The second type is completely opposite to the first, but almost as dangerous. These are people who, facing danger, begin excessive and pointless activity as if hoping that varying chaotic movements will give them a lucky break. Of course, if one has not witnessed it with one's own eyes, it is difficult to believe, but I have seen soldiers who, under artillery fire, begin to reorganise the sacks with their belongings, disassemble and reassemble their rifles or even polish their boots. Then there is the third type characterised by one of the two forms of behaviour that are most popular both with people and animals: it is those who seek to escape danger by running. Although such behaviour – even if it is caused by instinct rather than a conscious decision – usually seems more reasonable than the aforementioned, it doesn't mean that it's always the right one. Most often circumstances are such that a person has to appreciate the situation clearly enough to choose action by either running or selecting the fourth possibility, namely, to fight.

It is interesting that at the beginning, all four types are characterised by the same bodily reactions: your heart begins to race, you sweat and you feel tense. We can only guess at why the very next moment these identical signs should lead to such a variety of behaviours. Perhaps a day will come when scientists will figure it all out and even find some special medicine – a tincture or something else – that will protect people from the danger posed by the first two types of behaviour. That would mean a great gain in the art of war, unless we believe that this war will end all wars and people will become more reasonable. As for me, I have discovered that the first two types of behaviour are completely alien to me and I most often and willingly choose the last – attack.

I pulled the bayonet out of my boot and got ready to fight. I also had a lighter in my pocket. I had heard that wolves are afraid of fire, yet here that was no consolation, for there was no chance that I could hurriedly make any kind of decent flame in the wet forest. The wolves did not attack immediately. They seemed to wait and see how dangerous an opponent I was. And yet, albeit barely noticeably, they kept drawing nearer and I could begin to see the steam of breath on some.

Then one of the pairs of eyes moved and jumped at me. Drawing aside, I managed to brandish the bayonet, yet it only hit empty air. The wolf swung around – now I saw him quite well, for he was out of the shadows – and was preparing for a new leap. At the same time, I had to keep an eye on those who were still staring from behind the trees. Now I was beginning to suspect that it would not end well, but then rhythmical clatter was heard, the wolves froze and pricked their ears. I immediately realised that it was the narrow-gauge, coming from the direction of Dundaga. It was possible that it carried my pursuers, yet in this moment it represented my escape. The noise of its little steam engine and wheels was still rather distant, yet the wolves grew restless. When the wooden bridge began to rumble and the locomotive started down the slope towards us, the wolves scattered to all sides. So that I would not have to run across the rails in front of the train, I dropped down by the side of the road. Huffing, puffing, moaning and rattling, the train dragged past us at its snail's pace. It had only two carriages and the yelling of German drunks could be heard from one of them.

Once the train had vanished in the distance, I found myself alone again in the quiet stillness of the forest. Worried that the wolves might return, I decided to walk on the rails. It was doubtful that another train would chase after the one that just went by, nor could one go in the other direction any time soon. I started climbing the embankment and had to stop dead in my tracks. An elk was staring at me from above – and it was not just any kind of elk: to me he looked gigantic. It may be that the image was distorted by my exhaustion, the lost blood and recent agitation. A huge crown of forked antlers loomed on the elk's head, yet he seemed peacefully inclined. Having stared at me for a while, he turned slowly, looked back one last time and then walked into the forest in a stately manner.

No explanation is needed for the pack of wolves or the elk, of course. I simply happened to be in the forest at night, where the animals are at home. And yet, walking down the narrow railway, I wasted time coming up with all kinds of fantastic theories. Elks should perhaps be grateful to me for saving one of their kind from death. If the wolves were chasing them, as I was quite sure they were, my showing up made the wolves change their intentions and disrupted the hunt. And then it was possible that the big elk I had begun to call their noble leader had come to show his gratitude.

These thoughts were nothing but pure fantasy, because wild animals clearly don't possess any of the feelings we humans are familiar with. Even fear of death is unknown to them, for only a being fully conscious of itself as a living creature can fear its sudden non-existence. Unlike human beings, animals are motivated not by a fear of death but by a desire to live. And only when this desire becomes too weak, when the animal has been losing blood or strength, or is forced to submit to another's will to live, does the animal die. It differs from us. Sometimes it is not the physically superior who win, not the ones who have the greatest will to live, but those whose fear of death is lacking.

And here, as I walked, I got to contemplate the fate of my people. Is it not the case that the invaders from various countries, but particularly Germans, are like a pack of wolves who, their eyes burning, have always wanted to do us in and then feed on us? And all that we have lacked so far is not lots of grit – for that would have been my demise in my encounter with a dozen wolves – but a lucky break and a bit of unexpected help? Yes, now I was even ready to acknowledge that help had come from higher or even lower powers, for haven't we always considered the animal kingdom to be on a lower rung? It was only the chubby German sentry who kept haunting me – although an enemy, I had killed him as a private individual not exactly belonging to any army and after an armistice had been signed by all warring sides. Perhaps he simply lacked any outside power willing to protect him – no God, no wolf, no elk, no narrow-gauge railway and no starry heavens above had come to his rescue.

> "...spears will strike my young, free chest,
> A wily sword will cut off my head.
> Those damned bullets made of lead
> Will come and shatter my head..."

After so many incidents and my having got lost in the dead of the night, it took me a while to find the way the Usma forester had given me. It was early morning by the time I reached the house of the Pize forester Ozols. Woken by my persistent knocking, he opened the door armed with a hunting rifle, but noting my shabby appearance in the light of the paraffin lamp, he put the rifle aside and began to potter around. As he explained that I couldn't stay at his house because Germans were in the habit of coming and going as they wished, he turned off the lamp and took me in the complete darkness through the vegetable garden and away from the house, over the pasture and into the forest. He leaned down at a small, mint-covered hillock and vanished. I thought that perhaps, in my weak condition, my vision was deceiving me, but then I saw a light flashing right under my feet: there was a hole in the ground, the forester had descended on a narrow staircase into a bunker and turned on the lamp. Great skill had been put into its construction – there were no signs of moisture or mould on the walls or ceiling, and the floor was dry, white sand. By one wall there was a makeshift bed made of pinewood nailed together, and near it was a table and in the farthest corner a bucket with a lid.

"Not bad, eh? Really not bad," Ozols said with pride. "I made it myself. So that I have somewhere to go when the teeter-totters strike."

Putting the lamp on the table, the forester wanted to see about my wound. He did not pay any heed to my protestations that it was nothing serious. Now that there was light, I could take a good look at Ozols. He was one of those men who always look very sunburnt and grimy – his face was engraved with deep and dark wrinkles, a black-and-white beard bristled in all directions and, under his bushy eyebrows, bright eyes flashed and looked a little crazy. The light revealed my conditions. The sleeve was drenched with dark blood from top to bottom and, as I removed my clothes, the sight was quite appalling. My shirt-strip bandage had not helped much, because the bullet, entering at an oblique angle, had torn out a rather large piece of flesh from the elbow almost to the shoulder. No wonder that the wolves had smelt a nice morsel.

"Didn't I say so? Didn't I say so?" Ozols was huffing and puffing. "I know what it means to lose so much blood! I know, I shoot animals." Working together, we bandaged my arm as best we could, but it was clear that stitches were in order. "Stay here and sleep," he ordered. Then he put the lamp on the table and was on his way. "Wait and don't go anywhere. I'll be back soon."

He pushed shut the entrance to the bunker and I remained alone in the underground illuminated by the paraffin lamp. I lay down on the narrow bunk and wrapped myself in the white coat given to me by Fyodor Pavlovich. Even though winter was still far off, this was probably the first time that it served its purpose. And yet I was shaking with cold. I would have liked to doze off, but the exhaustion, the wounded arm and all the adventures of this day kept sleep at bay and continued to excite my imagination.

What had Ozols said about this place? Who are the teeters he mentioned? Was it some Liv word and he used it to call Germans names? What else could it be? I was sweating profusely, a fever had set in and all of my body was racked with pain except for the wounded arm. It was as if someone else had taken residence in my body, some creature that was gnawing at me from the inside and trying to break out.

I have no idea how long I tossed and turned until I heard the hatch open and two people come down the stairs. Ozols had brought someone with him. It was a man of about the same age, just very gaunt and tall. He had a thin, long, white goatee and an annoyed, even angry look in his eyes. I didn't really pay any attention at the time, but now it seems to me that he did not utter a word, just growled and mumbled to himself and, from time to time, ordered Ozols to do something by moving his head.

(Wave of the head.) Ozols lifted the lamp higher.

(Wave of the head.) Ozols pushed the lamp closer.

(Wave of the head.) Ozols handed him his bag.

Yet as far as I could tell, the oldster knew his trade no worse than doctors in any field hospital. He not only disinfected and stitched the wound, but even injected me with some morphine. It may be why my recollection of their departure is so muddled.

7 October
When I woke up I had no idea whether it was day or night-time, evening or morning. By the light of my lighter, I found and turned on the paraffin lamp. Next to it was a jug with water. My arm hurt of course, but overall, I felt much better. I tried to write down as precisely as possible what I had experienced the day before, yet I tired easily and fell asleep again.

I was awakened by Ozols, who had brought some bread and smoked fish. I had no appetite, but out of politeness I snacked a little and, as I did so, asked Ozols about the local situation. Upon retreating, the Russians had taken along the lights of the Pize and other seaside lighthouses. The Germans had replaced those with their carbide lamps.

"Now we have our own railroad!" Ozols chuckled and then became serious and grim again. "They're cutting down all our forests and taking them off to Ventspils. If they continue like this, all that remains will be one big swamp."

8 October
In my underground dwelling I couldn't distinguish day from night, nor could I tell whether I was alive or dead, awake or dreaming. This was brought home to me in the morning, although the thought that morning had come struck me only because I woke up. Somebody was standing by my bunk and had possibly stood there for some time. Yet it was neither Ozols, nor the doctor he had called. It was a woman!

It was so startling that I let my imagination run wild. First,

I got scared that I might be dead and this was something from the kingdom of the dead. Or I was on death's threshold and Death itself had rushed over to take me. I realised that she wasn't Death or from the kingdom of the dead, of course; I saw that she was a living being made of flesh and blood wrapped up in a plaid, and also rather attractive. As I found out soon enough, her name was Nēze and she was the god-daughter of old Ozols. He had to take care of some business with the Germans and she was supposed to take care of me in the meantime. Nēze was not particularly talkative and, if she said something, it was done in a quiet and melodic voice and with a questioning inflection at the end. She had brought me bread and a cup of milk.

When the girl left, my thoughts immediately turned to her, and these thoughts did not leave me the entire time I was awake. I began to contemplate the fact that through all this excitement and chaos I'd had no chance or interest to establish an acquaintance with any woman. Although I had chanced upon a few attractive faces in Russia, awareness of my precarious position had always prevented me even from introducing myself. Perhaps it was a mistake, I now mused, deep in thought about the bright features of Nēze. I tried to recall whether I had ever held the hands of a girl I loved or hoped to taste another pair of lips on my own.

9 October

Today I managed to have more of a conversation with Nēze. I was surprised at her sharp mind and political views. For a moment, I almost thought she was trying to convince me that only the Bolsheviks had some purchase on the truth. At the same time, I sensed that we were too different and, even though Nēze seemed very nice and sympathetic to me, we could never develop any feelings for each other. Indeed, we could consider each other opponents, and we only avoided open warfare because we both happened to be in the area controlled by the Germans. It seemed that

Nēze's godfather also did not share her views. I am convinced that in a different situation, Nēze would not have hesitated to declare me a class enemy and want to rid herself of me with no regret whatsoever. Would I too have behaved like that? Here we have to consider the fact that she was a young woman. Would I have been capable of killing her? What if my survival depended on it? Would I have acted as I did to the chubby German?

Only several years later did I find out that Nēze had met a sad fate even without my direct involvement. A month later, on the day when the German Kaiser Wilhelm II abdicated and a couple of days before the end of the First World War, she and her comrades had tried to destroy the German railroad near Lūžņas. It turned out that she was not just a young woman indoctrinated by Bolshevik propaganda, but an active Chekist.

The red fighters' plan was to blow up the rails, prevent German weapons and other war materials from being taken to Ventspils port and then use the seized arms to fight their political opponents and establish the rule of "workers and peasants" in Kurzeme. As it turned out, Nēze had her own scores to settle with that railroad. All of the women from the surrounding villages – both young and old – had been ordered by the Germans to participate in building the railroad and when Nēze told me about it, I heard the kind of hatred in her voice that many Latvians had accumulated over the course of several generations. Upon mentioning that greying fishermen's wives and old men had to lay down rails through swamps and thickets, Nēze turned red in the face, shook with fury and looked downright dangerous.

Yet one of the would-be saboteurs had turned out to be a traitor. The Germans had learnt of the plan well in advance and had ambushed the fighters at the railroad. The saboteurs attempted to fight and, as a result, most were shot. Nēze and another comrade were taken prisoner and brought to Ventspils, where they were interrogated and eventually shot. It's not clear who the traitor was. I have heard some argue that it was Nēze herself, and that she received her just reward. The revolution took great pleasure in devouring its own children. Whatever the facts of this matter, I realised once more that Death had been stalking me during that period.

12 October

I left Ozols and Nēze without saying goodbye so that I would not have to tell them of my plans and could thus avoid at least some of the suffering felt by strangers who had treated me kindly.

It was a rather warm and sunny day, and the entire forest had a golden glow to it, there was the scent of ferns, which had begun to decay, and my mind was filled with slightly melancholic, yet energetic thoughts. Sure, some of them were still preoccupied with the image of Nēze. In my pensive state, it occurred to me that I'd probably never forget her bright and determined countenance and would try to rediscover it in others.

To avoid further trouble, I had decided to stop pretending to be a reporter. Before setting out, I had modified my appearance a little, and in part it had changed on its own. Several days without shaving and washing in the underground dwelling, which was sooty from the paraffin lamp, had made me not only dirtier but also older.

I only took the things I needed most and left all the rest with Ozols along with a brief note. I also left the white winter coat given to me by Fyodor Pavlovich, the bayonet I had taken from the German, my papers acquired in Russia, a shaving kit and some other things whereby anyone who so wished could easily guess that I wasn't the person I was pretending to be. In the note, I thanked Ozols and asked him to keep my things, as well as expressed hope that some time later I would have a chance to come and retrieve them.

This has yet to happen and from time to time I have a thought that I should return there and see if something has been kept for me. But it must be Nēze's fate that has always prevented me from doing so.

I was wearing a tattered short sheepskin coat belted with a piece of rough string – Nēze had given me it for use as a blanket; my boots, on the other hand, were in such a pitiful state, despite having been mended several times, that no one would suspect that the person wearing them was an officer from the czarist Russian army. In one of the boots I had also concealed this journal.

Yet I continued to exercise caution. The road continued to run almost parallel to the German railway, which meandered around any sizeable hill, swamp and even dense cluster of trees. Once again I heard the train approach, had to hide in the forest by the roadside and wait for it to trundle by and disappear around the curve.

It couldn't have been far from Oviši when I saw a cart appear from a side road leading towards the sea. Since it was obvious that the driver wasn't German, I quickened my pace and caught up with him, a decrepit old man smoking a pipe and wearing a deerstalker shiny with age. He was taking home-made ropes to Ventspils, hoping to exchange them for paraffin, salt and other everyday needs. So we continued to plod on together.

"I'm old," he said, tapping on his pipe. "I don't have much time remaining, but I fret about the young ones. How are they going to live here under the Germans? That's worse than under the Russians. They don't care about anyone."

Astonishingly, this simple man from a fishing village had understood the very thing that I was told that same day by teacher Osis in his flat on Kuldīgas Street. When I was in Russia, Colonel B had urged me to get in contact with Osis, a fellow countryman of his. The teacher had not escaped in 1914, for he was still living with his very sick mother who was almost unable to move without help. He had also been able to avoid military service because he was bow-legged after a childhood bout of bone tuberculosis, which had been successfully treated right there in Ventspils, at a sanatorium run by Doctor Velyaminov. His mother had died, yet he continued to live in the very heart of Ventspils and observe the changes the Germans brought. And these were hardly limited to the monument erected to Kaiser Wilhelm near his house. Immediately upon entering the city, the Germans had appointed their own to all positions of standing and behaved as if it were their homeland. Yet, as the war dragged on, real panic ensued. Considering the war all but won, they saw Bolsheviks as their last enemy and all Latvians as Bolsheviks. For this reason and because most of Osis's students were now somewhere far away, he kept to himself, no longer conducted the choir (for there were no singers either) and mostly stayed at home, working on a Liv-Latvian dictionary for days on end.

As far as I know, he never finished that task and perished at the end of the Second World War.

"We're certainly not going to get any trust from the Germans or help with fighting the Bolsheviks," Osis said. "To German eyes, Latvians are Bolsheviks too, and those who even dare to dream about an independent Latvian state are semi-Bolsheviks. Thus they are Germany's enemies. And in a way, it's true. The only question is how to channel all this in another direction."

He likened the fate of the Latvians to that of the Livs, and with a certain amount of pathos, he said that a lack of awareness of our roots, advantages and chances may mean that we too would become an insignificant footnote in the history of the German Baltic Duchy.

15 October
The unusually early, rainy and chilly autumn has been replaced by an equally brief winter. I awoke to a strange

brightness, and had to go to the window before I realised that it came from the snow. Snow was falling in large, fluffy flakes and had already covered the ground in white. Where yesterday there had been disorder, grime, mud and city streets strewn with fallen leaves, there was pure white that gleamed in the sunlight, as if emphasising that finally this protracted warfare was coming to an end, and the time of mutual killing and the destruction of everything would be turned into the determination towards work that would inspire and produce instead of damage and impoverish.

For a couple of days I was alone in Osis's flat while he was in Riga. Doing the simple chores – firewood had to be brought in, the stove lit and meals prepared – I found solace in imagining that I lived in peacetime and that the flat with all of Osis's things belonged to me and I was living his life. I sat at his desk, looked out of his window, ate and drank from his china, read books I found in his bookshelf, listened to the ticking of his wall clock, but of course I could not be him. I am who I am.

Now I realised with displeasure that this period of war and chaos had not been without advantages for me. Orders from the high command, unexpected enemy manoeuvres, incredibly lucky coincidences and mortal danger of varying degrees have decided my fate for me. No doubt I have had some say in my own fate, yet it has been much less than it would have been in times of peace and prosperity. I have lived a life forced on me by external circumstances, and this realisation filled me with strange unrest and frustration. I know that I am not alone in this. This is what tends to happen during wars and other cataclysms, and you have to make your peace with it. Yet now I was disturbed and repelled not by the past but by the future, which suddenly spread before me like a field of white, undisturbed snow.

Having surrendered to fantasies of a peacetime life, I realised that I could not in fact picture it. To live in a flat like the one Osis had? To meet and marry a nice girl like Nēze?

None of it was possible of course! I was no Osis, I didn't work as a teacher and wasn't researching the Liv language. I didn't have his bow legs, thank God. I had to live my own life, and yet I didn't have the slightest idea of how to do it, how to continue and how to conduct my life to its end.

That's why I was happy for both Osis's return and the news he brought. He was excited to share the news that in Riga they were discussing the unification of the Latvian Provisional National Council set up in Valka and the Democratic Bloc of Riga. The National Council was going to dispatch its representative Zigfrīds Meierovics to England where he would talk with the ally's representatives about founding a free and independent Latvian state. True, some squabbling or competition was taking place between the council and the bloc, and representatives of both sides were apparently spreading ugly rumours amongst the English about their rivals. There was even some talk that German spies were active in the Democratic Bloc.

"There are as many parties as there are Latvians," Osis grumbled, though he still chuckled happily, for he was convinced that the opportunity to finally have our own country was very near.

And then I understood what I had to do. Everything fell into place, just like in a successful game. It turned out that all this time – for the most part unconsciously – I had been nearing this goal, and now it was time to take one final decisive step. If the conditions were this favourable for establishing a Latvian state, it was my duty to do everything within my power to help with the important job of state building. This thought was simultaneously so depressing and so uplifting that, in some peculiar way, it seemed to produce what religious people call an epiphany.

16 October

Early in the morning I said goodbye to Osis and went to the station. Snow was still coming down, yet it was warmer.

To avoid walking to the river crossing, I'd hired a cabby the day before, yet he did not show up, so I had to walk that considerable distance, slipping and sliding on the slushy streets.

As I stared into the darkened, grey black current of the Venta, I fancied that it was the line dividing my destiny: the war and all my past was left behind and on the opposite bank, my future goals and achievements could be seen. I must say that my optimism slackened once I got to the station and found out that I could hope for a train only in the evening at the earliest. To cross the river again and walk all the way back to Osis's place in this weather was not a tempting thought and thus I joined a group of other would-be travellers and spent almost half a day idling around the station stove.

At around four in the afternoon rumour spread that some cargo train would have two carriages for passengers attached and would arrive before seven in the evening. But then to our great amazement, it was announced that a carriage – a single one – had already been coupled to a train and was about to depart. A great panic set in and everyone rushed across the snow-covered rails to the far end of the train and tried to secure the best seats for themselves. It turned out, however, that there was no reason for this excitement: the car remained half-empty, the train didn't budge for another two hours, and all this time we had to freeze in the absence of any heat.

19 October

I have returned to Riga both happy and sad. From the train I'd seen a large flock of birds in a field, where they had landed to rest their wings before the long journey to warmer climes. I immediately thought of all the Latvians still wandering the Russian wastes far from their homeland.

It was the first thing that struck me in Riga. Although it was nice to see familiar places and walk on familiar streets, it was sad to notice how empty they now were and how quickly various changes the Germans imposed had taken root. They had put up an ugly monument to their "home guard" in the square where the regional court stands. I soon found out that the locals had quickly named the thing "Wooden Fritz".

"Riga's face is regaining its Germanic features," *Rigasche Zeitung* enthused, and indeed the Germanic face was staring back at us everywhere. Day and night, loud music was heard non-stop in pubs, all-night establishments and restaurants – just like there was no end to the bottles of vodka, beer and champagne. Shops had been plundered and boarded up, yet partying and ostentation looked even more striking against this background. Fine suits, resplendent officers, ladies' dresses made by Jewish seamstresses in Berlin, garish courtesans flocking to the city from all over, hunting dogs of unheard-of pedigrees, the names of German newspapers shouted by Latvian paperboys, noisy and violent German films at the cinema, sentimental German plays in the theatres, German books direct from the printer's and the conviction, thought or uttered in every German dialect, that Latvians do not deserve their own culture or land – for it is they, the Germans, who own everything.

The signs everywhere and only in German were in complete opposition to what we had recently experienced under the tsar. Opposition, yes, and yet it was so familiar! Now it seemed a distant past, but just a few years ago when the war had only just begun, all German signs were being painted over and everything was rewritten in Russian. German street names on postcards were erased and you could be detained for conversing in German on the street or on the tram.

Now it has all changed in the opposite direction. "Our historic mission in Latvia will be fulfilled once the German branch grafted on to this rootstock develops into a most magnificent flower," wrote a Kurzeme nobleman. Signs in

Russian are nowhere to be seen, and Russian and Latvian are rarely heard. As I noticed already at the station and soon enough in the city, even many Latvians consider it appropriate, or at least safer, to converse amongst themselves in German – as best they can. Anywhere you go you are first greeted in German and only if you reply in Latvian, the person greeting you seems to be a bit startled and then reluctantly switches to Latvian.

In light of all this, I was beginning to understand those who had been developing the idea of our own Latvian state. We will never be able to establish a great power with colonies and other associated perquisites, and much has been written about the famous Latvian attempts to colonise Brazil, Siberia and other far-off lands. There's not much we can produce or grow in our country to base our economy on. For that reason, the main, if not the only, point to having our own country is our language. We have the right to a country where we can talk and write freely in Latvian. Irrespective of whether you're Russian, German, Polish or Jewish, here we'll address you in Latvian, whereas elsewhere Latvians do not and cannot enjoy such a possibility or right. So whether or not you are a patriot of your country, you'll be judged first and foremost by whether you know the Latvian language, and not by your origins or ancestry.

26 October

In the late morning I decided to walk to the estate to visit my mother and father. It was windy yet warm and sunny, and I enjoyed walking, so I decided to take the longer route around Lake Ķīšezers. On my way, I made a detour through Vecmīlgrāvis and passed the temperance society building, Ziemeļblāzma Manor, which was built by Augusts Dombrovskis. The accomplishments of this man deserve the greatest admiration, and the story about how an execution squad tied Dombrovskis to a tree and burnt down the original "Ziemeļblāzma" building before his very eyes makes my heart sink with sadness and frustration. Now I was glad to see that the new building constructed of cement bricks and iron, which was unveiled shortly before the war, stood tall and proud like a cliff in the middle of the slightly neglected park. True, it was sad to see that Germans had taken over the building, but now I was convinced that it would not be that way for long.

It is time for Latvians to abandon their philosophy of "I walked through a silver grove, and did not break a single twig," which is supposedly encoded in our folk song. I had often thought of this and now, as I passed "Ziemeļblāzma", I thought of it once again. Probably because Dombrovskis had eagerly supported the efforts by Krišjānis Barons to collect and publish Latvian folk songs. It is a well-known fact that hundreds and thousands of songs were sent to him and, for some reason, no one was surprised at this huge amount.

Andrejs Pumpurs made a diligent effort to fill the supposed gap that Latvians had where other peoples have all kinds of epic song or *epos*. So he wrote "Lāčplēsis", the Bearslayer. And now it sometimes occurs to me that Krišjānis Barons perhaps took upon himself a similar, but even more difficult and grand enterprise, namely, not only to collect and organise Latvian folk songs, but also to compose them.

It is no secret that we have not had too many educated people. Their numbers increased considerably only in the second half of the previous century, particularly at the very end of it. And this is why I cannot figure out who the diligent collectors of the Latvian folk songs would have been, and who would have sent those songs in.

This may just be my suspicious nature, exacerbated by all I had gone through during the war.

18 November

The auditorium of the Latvian Opera House, formerly the Russian Theatre, was so crowded and there was so much pushing and shoving at the door that I could barely get in. It was already much later than the scheduled start time of 4 p.m., yet nothing had happened. Something on the stage was being fixed and tidied up. With much effort, I elbowed my way to the farthest corner of a box on the left side and, as could have easily been guessed, had to watch the entire event on my feet. Many people were standing and it seemed that many of them had done their part or even shed blood to help our nation get to this point. This is not to diminish the merits of those who sat on the lavishly adorned stage. About thirty moustachioed and bearded men sat there under a large red-white-red flag amongst lush greenery, and it would not be an exaggeration to say we were in the presence of almost all of the best and strongest that Latvia can offer. Sitting in the middle, Gustavs Zemgals, Marģers Skujenieks, Kārlis Ulmanis and Miķelis Valters in his white spats were of course the most prominent. I also recognised Jānis Akuraters. The names of those I didn't know were revealed to me by a student, Andrejs, who had been pushed up against me.

I was saddened by many of those who sat in the stalls. They were sitting there with long faces – to put it very mildly. It seemed that they had only come out of curiosity to find out if they could gain anything from the newly established Latvian state and if so, what exactly that would be. They were the ones who'd been doing quite well under the Germans, Russians or some other power. I didn't detect any faith in their faces – only calculation. They must have been the same people who'd been so eager to turn themselves into Germans when the Germans were in charge and would become Russians again, should the Russians return. This observation depressed me and made wonder what chances of survival our country had – particularly because of the contrast between the mood of these people and that of both those who sat onstage and those who stood and felt the importance of what was taking place with all their heart.

And yet the event resembled a theatre performance staged for the benefit of a bored audience gathered in the centre of a city occupied by an alien power – an audience who may even have arrived in anticipation of something entirely different. Almost every word pronounced from the stage fell into the audience as if into a bottomless vessel and died without gaining much resonance. Maybe the beginning of the ceremony was at fault when, a little after 4.30, the applause died down and Zemgals announced somewhat timidly that he would open the meeting of the National Council instead of Čakste, seeing how the latter had not yet arrived. After the minutes of yesterday's council meeting were read, Zemgals announced that all power in Latvia was now vested with the National Council and that Kārlis Ulmanis was to head the provisional government. All of this was received with applause.

"It will not be an easy task, but I am strengthened by my awareness of the power of the Latvian nation," Ulmanis said to enthusiastic applause by the audience. "All citizens, regardless of their nationality, are invited to help, for the rights of all peoples will be guaranteed in Latvia. It will be a democratic and just state in which no oppression or injustice will be tolerated!"

The applause after this speech was even more enthusiastic and then it was time for the Opera Choir, with Pauls Jozuus as conductor, to sing the new anthem of the fledgling state: "God Bless Latvia!". Again I was overcome by a peculiar feeling, for almost no one amongst the seated audience – although now on their feet – sang along. Perhaps they were afraid; perhaps they couldn't quite believe that now we would be the ones in charge. I was one of them, and this was rather unpleasant – you are there at the moment your country is born, you hear its anthem but find yourself unable to sing along. In a possible attempt to get round this awkward moment or perhaps teach the lyrics of the unfamiliar song to the audience, the anthem was sung several more times and I noticed that the audience in the stalls was getting annoyed and impatient at having to stand for so long.

It may have been from the lack of fresh air that towards the end of the event I began to fantasise. I pictured all of us present as trees with roots, trunks, branches and leaves. Many had very deep and strong roots that reached into our common past where they were nourished by experience, wisdom, rigour and strength accumulated over many centuries. At that moment, they were like solid trunks, yet their branches bearing leaves and fruit reached far into the future. I saw such trees in the men on the stage, I spotted them in the choir and there were quite a few amongst those of us who stood. The picture of the seated audience was much different. They were half-toppled stumps, fungus-covered remnants, misshapen, crooked saplings barely alive in a swamp; they were brush, underwood and all kinds of stubble. They all lacked something. Even if they still possessed roots, their trunks and branches were already withering, wasting away or were plagued with pests. Some were wrapped in white webbing woven by nasty caterpillars, and others were covered in bedbug-shaped vermin that chewed their buds and leaves. Those who had a trunk were lacking roots. And then there were those who had neither roots nor trunks, only entangled, protruding branches.

I continued to watch the audience as it was beginning to disperse. I heard some say that tomorrow's performance *The Flying Dutchman* was not to be missed, and was to be conducted by Reiters himself. Much to my surprise, everyone left very quickly and soon I was alone and exposed to the chilly wind at the front of the theatre building. The fathers of the new country may have gone to celebrate the event in a more private setting, yet I was astonished by the speed with which it was all over.

What I saw in the auditorium and observed at the theatre door have remained impressed on my mind. As the guests said their hasty goodbyes and congratulated one another by shaking hands, I noticed that the fingers on many a hand were crooked, stiff and unmoving as the stumps of withered branches. This made me think of all the times I'd recently had dealings with such people. Up to now, I had considered this affliction some sign of spiritual superiority. It almost seemed like a secret handshake uniting those who were nurturing in their hearts the dream of a country where their children and grandchildren could put down roots. Now I realised that I had been mistaken. These were the same old stumps and stubbles, the crooked pieces of the wood of humanity, which, like some shavings thrown into the sea, like some doomed "flying Dutchmen", floated through the fog wherever the current was carrying them and worried only about their puny gains. For the rest of their lives they will keep their fingers crossed. No promise, no oath they give will be true; they will be able to lie and not fear punishment, for they will always have a falsehood hidden in their pockets. And there were many of them. Many more than the rest.

It may have been simply from the cold, but at that very moment the fingers of my right hand grew numb and momentarily seemed to cramp, and in my fright I almost ended up under a cab. I did not want to become one of them. I wanted to resist them. I would rather cut off my hand or do myself in than become one of them. I wanted to protect our Latvian state.

Throughout the war, I asked myself again and again: "What would I be ready to die for?" It was clear that death could come at any time, and therefore I wanted to understand what would make my death feel like a meaningful event and not just an accident of fate. On that day, I finally began to see the possibility of such an event. Our country and state became a single entity – an idea we'd nurtured for decades. They could not exist without each other. And it is impossible to love one of them and not love or not care for the other. If the state were in danger, we wouldn't be able to hide in some safe Noah's Arc and survive the danger. We would have to fight to the last man, because surrender or abandonment of our country would mean no state and no Latvia.

Today I made a firm decision: I'd rather die than abandon Latvia to its fate, for my roots belong to this land – I'm no accidental resident, but a part of the Latvian people. I am not some rootless shrub, mushroom or a rotting fungus-covered stump; I want to put down roots, sprout, grow and bring benefit to my country.

At this juncture I had to ask myself: "What can I do for my country?" And the answer was clear: first we must get rid of the Germans.

And what next? How could I be most useful? At this moment, I can become anything at all. The past has lost its meaning, the future is empty and has yet to be built, and the only important things are the decisions we make here and now. Neither I nor anyone else will ever have this kind of moment. Shall I take on a government job? Continue with the military? Make use of the knowledge I acquired at the polytechnic and am beginning to forget? Turn to commerce – perhaps start an import/export business? Open a restaurant or a pastry shop? (I don't know why but confectionery and bread baking seem to me the activity most characteristic of peacetime.)

It was now completely dark: because of the chaos and shortages, street lights did not function and even candles in windows of apartment buildings were few and far between. I let instinct and my hearing guide me as I walked; the wind whistled loudly in the trees at the edge of the esplanade and, from time to time, the creaking of branches sounded like the sorrowful weeping of women and children.

And then I thought I could see something, perhaps human figures, moving in the inky darkness. At first they seemed to be dangerous, but soon I discovered that they couldn't see me or feel my presence – or rather they weren't even capable of seeing or feeling. They appeared to be separating from the tree trunks and were coming towards me slowly and heavily. Or were the trees themselves turning into ghosts of human semblance in my wind-inspired imagination? I smelt decay, which was nothing unusual – the ground was covered with fallen leaves – and yet this smell disturbed me. It was not just composed of rotting maple and oak leaves but also pungent mildew, moisture-drenched leather, weapon oil, smut, soot, smoke, heavy soil, blood-soaked cloth and the sickly-sweet stench of bodies. Plodding steps were rustling the leaves, the exhausted walkers could barely lift their feet and it seemed that they were condemned to this wandering for all eternity. Now I could pick out some of them – they were figures dressed in grey greatcoats: some dragged themselves along on their own, others could move only when supported by their comrades. There were some whose arms or legs were missing, several had no head, but in between there were plenty of those who lacked any visible wounds – it's just that their faces were grey and gaunt, and instead of eyes they had black, empty sockets.

And I recognised them! They were all my comrades who had fallen at different times. These were men who had gone to fight and meet their death without knowing or hoping that this wonderful day for our people would arrive – even though it may feel more like a dark and ghost-filled night. They were dead, whereas I, by some incomprehensible fluke, was alive. Was it not the ghost-time of the year, so venerated by our ancestors?

If only it were possible, I would have respectfully asked them all to come to my home, treated them to whatever little I have and then allowed them to rest and get warm. Yet it was obvious that these men were no longer in need of food, drink or sleep; they were driven by an endless and eternal yearning: "What was it for?" But in this too I was of no assistance. No one was. I could yell at the top of my voice, scream until I was completely hoarse and try to tell them that their deaths were not in vain, that they made a great and important sacrifice for the living, but I wouldn't be heard. There's no gift of speech that allows us to communicate with the past. And we have no chance of finding out about the future, for who knows what we could see, hear or feel there.

My ghastly vision was interrupted by a flash of blinding light. In the dense darkness of night, it was like lightning, but much brighter. It offered no illumination though, because the light was soon replaced by impenetrable, black darkness and silence so absolute that for a brief moment I thought I had become both blind and deaf. Yet my senses gradually returned and I was again alone in the unlit street. There were no longer any phantoms, apparitions or ghosts.

Even after returning home and lighting the paraffin lamp and a candle, I continued to wonder about the light and the ensuing darkness. I couldn't read in the poor light with my excited state of mind. Man is the kind of creature who sooner or later begins to consider home any place where he has ended up passing the time, whether willingly or not, and regardless of the kind of place home has become: furnished rooms, prison, or a Bedouin tent in the desert. One could say that home is where you are. But what if these two weak lights went out? What if the entire city went completely dark? If one could not see the world, could we still say that it exists? We see only colours because they're forms of light, and we hear sounds because we are surrounded by atmosphere. We can capture the subject of smell and other senses only because everything is composed of atoms. And it all takes place in our minds, in our consciousness. At the moment when darkness set in, when the atoms ceased moving, everything would stop. There would be nothing. That's all.

V. ROOTS

30 October
Today we raked the leaves on both sides of the house for the second time. Some are still hanging on to the oak branches, but that's nothing. The wind will tear them off and blow them away. A storm has been forecast for the evening. I cut the grass on the terrace side for the last time. I had filled the mower's fuel tank, so I had to cut the grass on the other side of the pond as well, but I didn't bother with the meadow the wild boar had dug up.

In the afternoon, the arborist came. I didn't even know that there was such a profession. A kind of a tree surgeon. Apparently, there are quite a few of them in Latvia these days – with the appropriate education, certificates and websites. I wanted him to take a look at both of our oaks. There are dry branches on their crowns, which are beyond our reach. I was pleased to notice that our oaks made an impression even on the tree expert. He looked them over and said that they were in good health. Yet he did notice some branches under stress on the gate side.

"Branches under stress?" I repeated. It turns out that a tree begins to grow them at times when it feels something worrisome – the level of groundwater shifting, soil composition changing or some such. But we were not to worry about these stressed branches, for the oak had grown them a couple of years ago. It was probably when the water level suddenly rose, which prompted a return to that thought – well, maybe not the one about whether plants have consciousness, but whether or not they feel something. I remembered once reading that the composition of the soil influences plants and they influence those who consume them. Possibly, it even determines some congenital diseases or some character traits. The trees themselves are incapable of walking and thinking. Tied to the ground by their one "leg", they trust their consciousness and thoughts to someone else. Wine is a good example. It too is influenced by the *terroir* in which the vines have grown, which determines the taste of the wine as well as its impact on our flesh and soul. What if, at the moment when a person, under the influence of wine, begins to babble, it were the vine that's desperately trying to speak through him or her? Or is it perhaps the rocks?

1 November

We returned to the city only late at night. The previous night's storm hadn't done much damage, but the power was out in the whole area, and this was followed by the phones. Tedis's dog wandered over to our house, but Tedis himself had been in the village cemetery for almost two years now. The dog wandered outside the house but could not be persuaded to come in. So he stayed outside throughout the storm. Finally around noon the next day, the power was restored. The mobile-phone transmitter came to life even later.

It was now an ordinary city morning. I looked at my mobile's screen several times, moved the previously set waking time half an hour forward and fell asleep for a moment, then woke up, looked at Twitter and moved the alarm ahead again. Then I scrambled out of bed and went to the kitchen; it was sunny even though in the bedroom it had seemed that it was overcast with ominous black clouds and rain. I switched on the electric kettle and measured some instant coffee into cups. I looked at the outdoor thermometer, then went to take a leak and brush my teeth, and in the meantime the water had boiled and I could pour it on to the coffee. I noticed that the neighbours on the other side of the courtyard had not let their cat out on the balcony. I took the three parts of the juicer out of the cupboard, put them together, chose two grapefruits, washed them, put a paper towel by the juicer, cut the grapefruits one after the other and juiced each half, poured the resulting juice into a glass, shook the dregs and the remaining juice into another glass and immediately proceeded to gulp it down. I washed the juicer parts and put them on the rack to dry, threw out the paper towel and noticed that the garbage can was full. I removed the full bag, tied it up and took it out to the hallway, picked up the coffee, sat down at the table, opened the computer, looked at the same websites I look at every morning in addition to Twitter, and finally began to read a lengthy article about a recently invented area of research – post-humanitarian sciences.

The representatives of this science apparently are trying to correct the picture of the world distorted over centuries by human anthropocentrism and narcissism. One branch of this science is speculative realism, which allows that even inanimate objects – such as a cameras, rocks, pillowcases, canvas coats, animation heroes, power lines, cell towers and of course trees – possess a kind of autonomy that, short of attaining consciousness, is nevertheless a set of features that allow us to perceive these seemingly inanimate objects not as things but as "agents" involved in various processes related to time and space. Such authors as Francis Hallé in his book *In Praise of Plants*, Jeffrey Jerome Cohen in *Animal, Vegetable, Mineral* and Michael Marder in his recent book *Plant-Thinking: A Philosophy of Vegetal Life* are trying to lend scientific gravitas to this seemingly esoteric direction of research.

According to Marder, even though it would be an exaggeration to say that an oak, for example, possesses some sort of experience of its surroundings, this doesn't mean that an oak is incapable of thought and thinking in ethical categories. This is a train of thought common in Latvian folk poetry: "I walked through a silver grove, but did not break a single twig," or "The river carried an oak with all the bees." This kind of animism completely contradicts Heidegger's Aristotelian conviction that a rock has no idea about the world and an animal's understanding of it is rather rough, whereas human beings close themselves up in their separate world. Marder notes that people tend to refer to plants only metaphorically: "family tree", "the crooked wood of humanity", "an apple doesn't fall far from the tree", "to push up daisies" and the like. At the same time, we don't even seem to notice that we eat, drink and smoke plants and trees; we encounter them in every piece of paper or furniture; we sleep on them and wear them; we live in houses made of wood and go on sea voyages in wooden ships; we bury our dead in wooden caskets and we knock on wood to prevent disaster.

2 November

My last name comes from my great-grandfather. He was Polish, participated in the mutiny by Polish noblemen, was deported to Siberia and then met my Latvian great-grandmother in Lithuania. After the revolution of 1905, my grandfather was tried in Vilnius and exiled to Siberia. At the end of the First World War, he was conscripted and entered Riga along with other Latvian riflemen in the early 1920s, after the founding of the Latvian state. Here he married my grandmother who was German. And apparently my grandfather too, when in his cups, liked to speak some German.

My great-grandmother on my mother's side was Russian, the daughter of a gardener on an estate. My Latvian great-grandfather met her in Russia. When the gardener's wife died, the owner of the estate, a general in the tsar's army, took the girl in and brought her up as one of his own. So my great-grandmother was also a general's stepdaughter. My mother's father, my grandfather, was picked off the street by the Germans during the Second World War and sent to do forced labour in Denmark. He died in Sweden without ever getting back to Latvia.

I was born not in Latvia but in the Latvian SSR, and my parents are Latvians. They were born in independent Latvia but later were forced to become citizens of the Soviet Union. I am Latvian. My language is Latvian. My country is Latvia. I have never doubted any of that. And I am also aware that it has not been within my power to somehow influence or change any of this. By some miracle the locals had found the letters my grandfather had put in a bottle and thrown into the sea when the German ship was passing Kolka, and they sent them to my grandma. Possibly they were Livs. That's simply how it was. I was yet to be born. That's my family tree.

I think it was Augustine who wrote that fear of death is unfounded, if by death we mean a time when we will no longer exist. It would be equally wrong, he stated, to fear the time when we did not yet exist – the time before we were born. This thought is actually of earlier provenance, for even Aristotle and others wrote that it is foolish to worry about and be afraid of things that are not within our power to change or prevent.

The ethnic identity and a sense of belonging to a state, which in our case seems to simultaneously be and not be at the basis of our national identity, I have always considered similarly unavoidable. You are like a tree. Wherever you are planted or wherever you ended up as a seed, you have to grow. It is the same with time. You have to live in the time you have been thrown into, whereas no one has been provided with the opportunity to observe or even fully imagine life in a different era. No one chooses one's parents or place of birth, and this is probably worth keeping in mind when thinking not only about ourselves but also our children and grandchildren.

Could it ever have crossed my grandmother Theophilia's mind that none of her grandchildren, great-grandchildren and now even great-great-grandchildren would be Germans and most of them wouldn't know a word of German? It probably didn't.

4 November

Our last trip to the countryside in the year, followed by our return to the city, is always filled with sadness. Even before the first snow, it reminds us that another year has passed. All we have to do is store the freezer bags with the last sautéed mushrooms, and darkness can begin. When I was a child, I always looked forward to winter and, although it was cold and I disliked winter sports, the first snow was a major event. These memories are not romanticism; to me, it is not an inevitably lost time to which I would wish to return. I remember the frozen balls of snow sticking to the fluff of my knitted trousers and woollen mittens: I can still smell the scent of wet clothes as I came home; I remember the huge mounds of snow shovelled to the side of the yard (it's been years since I've seen any that high); I remember the two-storey snow house with three or even four rooms built near one end of the house by the cherry tree (around it, in fact), yet I do not miss any of this. Well, maybe the forked cherry tree, which we used to climb in summer and pick out pieces of yellow resin that could be chewed like gum. I do remember that taste.

Now, winter to me is an encumbrance to be borne with reluctant tolerance or even something dangerous. The fear of winter is of course related to a well-concealed fear of death. After two car accidents experienced in winter and many incidents where I have barely avoided larger or smaller disasters, it seems that our winters, with their long black nights and days that last for only a few hours, are the time when Death is stalking us. The spirits of the dead may become restless in autumn, in the ghost season, but Death itself usually wanders around already after our Memorial Day, after the last candles in the cemetery have gone out and a black, opaque darkness has descended upon the earth. If I'm not mistaken, statistics suggest that more people die here in winter than in other seasons. And it's not just blizzards, icy roads, accidents on slippery sidewalks or pneumonia that are to blame.

While I was putting mushrooms into the freezer, I heard on the radio that during some construction work in Liepāja, they found the remnants of a wooden water main. Trees have the good sense to not overtax themselves in winter: they doze off to resume life with newly restored energy in spring. And even buried in the ground they are preserved and can tell us something even many centuries after they have been cut down, shaped and put to use.

7 November

"When a mushroom picker returns from the forest with a basketful of mushrooms, he's sure that the basket indeed contains mushrooms. He also remembers how carefully he had to separate them from the soil or even cut them with a knife in order not to damage the mushrooms' 'roots'. Yet this is far from the truth…" This is what Ferdinands Erdmans Štolls wrote in his excellent book *The Mushrooms of Latvia* as early as 1934. "If we were to lift the mossy ground cover somewhere in the forest, we'd see a thick network stretching between the roots and the ground. This network is formed by rather substantial strings and tiny threads resembling a spider's web. This is the mycelium which, branching to all sides, has expanded underground; it is the true mushroom."

Today I watched a documentary in which professor Suzanne Simard spoke about the mycelium as a kind of network used for mutual communication between trees in the forest. Electrical or light impulses carry information over telephone or Internet cables, but trees apparently use molecules of carbon dioxide to the same end. In this communication and in the life of trees in general, the so-called mother trees play an important role. Using a technical simile, one could say that mother trees are like servers that support the functioning of the entire computer network and provide the opportunity to connect to less important trees as well.

10 November

An argument broke out late in the night between two of our friends we were visiting, after quite a lot of wine had been drunk. I have no idea how it began, for we started paying attention only when voices were already raised.

"I see how they're coming on to the scene. In increasing numbers. Who are the best Latvian poets? Amongst the best contemporary Latvian poets are Russians from 'Orbita'! And what about theatre directors? Nastavshev, Petrenko... One after another. And there'll be more! They'll squeeze us out!"

"Who's going to squeeze you out of what exactly? They were born in Latvia, they live and work here, and they're our poets and our directors."

"No, they're not. They're Russians!"

"So what? Some of them are my friends. And Hanin, by the way, is Jewish."

"See, there's the problem!"

"What difference does it make – Russians, Germans or Jews? They're from Latvia!"

"But there is a difference! They're not Latvians and they're squeezing us out."

"How are they doing that?"

"A big nation squeezing out little ones. And you can never know what they have up their sleeves and what they will do if..."

"I don't know, I don't think that it's all that important for the young generation..."

"Exactly! There are no principles, no ideas about national

pride, about what makes a nation. And that'll be the end of us."

"And why is it so important to you?"

"What do you mean?"

"Why does it bother you so much?"

"I am simply worried about the future of our Latvian nation! The question is whether we will or will not be here in a few generations. And if it continues like this, then it's clear that there'll be nothing left of us."

"What will continue? We are a part of the European Union, NATO and God knows what else…"

"Yes, of course. Exactly. That too."

"But why does it worry you? You'll not experience it."

"What? You have a daughter. Is it all the same to you what language she'll speak?"

"She already speaks Latvian. She is Latvian. Yet I know that it's not up to me to determine what language she'll speak and who her children and grandchildren will be."

"Well, it's not all the same to me! And I am worried. Soon we'll meet the same fate as the Livs. And who did them in? The Russians!"

"Wait a minute, wasn't it Ulmanis who did that? And you shouldn't forget that before Ulmanis's coup the parliament had three official working languages: Latvian, German and Russian."

"But the Russians put a finishing touch to it! When the Soviet Army came in and closed off the Kurzeme seaside…"

"But no one is trying to do us in now."

"We will do it ourselves. We're already doing it. We're letting them do us in. Look at the Estonians…"

"Leave the Estonians out of it. What do you propose should be done? Shoot everyone you don't like?"

"Yes. Yes!"

"That sounds like Rumbula. We don't like the Jews – shoot them! We don't like the Russians – shoot them! All we have to do is find someone to blame for everything."

"Okay, okay!"

"So only we are not to blame for anything, right?"

"I didn't say that..."

"So if a Russian is a better theatre director or poet than you, he's to blame, right? It makes so much sense to just sit there and shoot the breeze and babble about how everything is really bad, and not do anything oneself. Not even try. For there's no point in trying. It's all clear anyway. All these others are to blame. And first and foremost because they've tried to do something, are doing it and – miracle of miracles! – are successful at it. Where are your productions, films, poetry, anything else? Nowhere. And if there's something that will do us in, it's this kind of thinking – if it hasn't already done so."

Both of them are our friends, we have known them and their views for a long time, and yet there was something so frightening in their quarrel that we did not feel like talking or even thinking about it. We walked home in silence.

[drawing]

Thinking about the conversation we heard yesterday, I remembered the essay "Border People" by the British historian Tony Judt in which he considered the notion and understanding of identity: "Undergraduates today can select from a swathe of identity studies: 'gender studies', 'women's studies', 'Asian-Pacific-American studies' and dozens of others. The shortcoming of all these para-academic programs is not that they concentrate on a given ethnic or geographical minority; it's that they encourage members of that minority to study themselves – thereby simultaneously negating the goals of a liberal education and reinforcing the sectarian and ghetto mentalities they purport to undermine. ... As so often, academic taste follows fashion. These programs are byproducts of communitarian solipsism: today we are all hyphenated – Irish-Americans, Native Americans,

157

African-Americans, and the like. Most people no longer speak the language of their forebears or know much about their country of origin, especially if their family started out in Europe. But in the wake of a generation of boastful victimhood, they wear what little they do know as a proud badge of identity: you are what your grandparents suffered."

Should I perhaps consider calling myself a Latvian of Cracow Polish origin? Father recalls that once we'd even had a family crest. Or maybe I am a Latvian of Riga German origin? Really fancy, but I don't feel like that at all.

I am here.

11 November, Lāčplēsis Day

At least one language dies every couple of weeks – that is when the last native speaker of a language passes away. At least half of the living languages today are used by fewer than 10,000 speakers, one-fourth are spoken by fewer than 1,000. Of the approximately 7,000 living languages over forty per cent are on the verge of extinction.

Yes, I know, as far as languages, traditions, histories are concerned – all of this can be purposefully planted into the next generation's mind: it can be taught. The experience of exile Latvians is a good example. I have been in the centres set up in various countries, I have seen the libraries accumulated there and have heard stories about selfless participation in Saturday schools and the efforts of determined parents to take their children to these schools.

Amongst the émigré Latvians there have been those who've considered it their duty to teach Latvianness to their children, and there have been those who have not seen much point to doing so. And I'm afraid that with each new generation, this desire diminishes.

18 November

Before our departure, my parents came for a visit. Even though the weather was shitty and my mother had difficulty walking, we took a short walk and then looked for a place to get warm. Mum and Dad recalled that once, after looking at an exhibition at "Arsenāls", we went down to the basement café at the National Theatre. There was a lot of activity around the theatre – I guess the final preparations were being made for the solemn event in the evening. The café was open and there were no customers there.

Upon seeing us, the guy behind the counter quickly hid the menu with the warm lunch courses – they were meant only for the actors and other theatre people. We had to choose between a few sorts of pies and pastries. My parents were fine with it, particularly my mother. As a result of some childhood trauma, she has always exercised caution when faced with food that has not been prepared at home. Looking at my father and mother, I had to think about their different origins and, likely, different heritage. They are like two different worlds: Father is ready to eat anything put in front of him, whereas Mother eats only what she knows and has tried before.

The built-in separation of classes has been retained more clearly in the opera house than in the National Theatre. The people sitting in the stalls are prevented from mixing with those sitting in the dress circle and government boxes or, for that matter, with those on the upper balconies, for each group gets to its seats by a different staircase. It may be that social life and its peculiarities, always supposing these still exist, are the main feature of class differences. From time to time, I've wondered how it could be that my parents have absolutely no friends. In other countries, I've observed with interest men and women in their seventies and eighties meeting every day in cafés or pubs near their homes, and it seems like they never feel lonely and they never lack someone to chat to. My father and mother do not know how to do it, even though they complain of loneliness and so many of their crowd of relatives have moved away and are often out of reach. Wouldn't it have been better if everyone had settled near each other? This has to be the Latvian peasant attitude, the individual farmstead kind of thinking which, amazingly enough given the motley origins of my ancestors, has infected even my family.

The previous evening, I had read about the time before the First World War. Ford's first assembly line, Igor Stravinsky's "Sacre du printemps", Kazimir Malevich's "Black Square", Marcel Proust's *Du côte de chez Swann*, the Paris law permitting the tango to be danced, Vilhelms Ķuze's first chocolate bars in Riga – it all took place in 1913, only one year before the great catastrophe occurred. Everywhere in the world, it was a time of great expectations, self-confidence, activity and growth. Prussia's capital Berlin was a flourishing metropolis with not only electric street lights but also electric trams. The number of telephones was said to be eight times that of London, not to mention such a backward and remote place as Rome. Berlin's streets were immaculate and the Berliners' faces must have been equally scrubbed and shiny – their lives literally conducted by the clock, as dinner was always at 8 p.m., concluded with a shot of something strong followed by a deep slumber. Advertisements in the London press invited residents to set out on a journey to such exotic places as Sudan, promising comfort in "express steamers and luxury train carriages". New York replaced Great Britain's capital as the world's largest port, and Argentina was still one of the richest countries. People enjoyed life and faced the future with confidence. They did not spot anything to worry about. The English politician Norman Angell was of the opinion at the time that no great war would ever begin, because countries are too interconnected by close economic ties. Oswald Spengler, known for his musings about the decline of the West, was considered a miserable pessimist.

On reading this, I realised that our lives are not so different from the deluded ones of 1913. Even though we lost the independence won in 1918 and lived for many decades under an alien power, we are used to peace. Even after the end of the Second World War, a number of wars were fought and the Soviet Union was involved in several of them, yet they all took place far away. The Latvian peasant probably thought in similar ways about the Russo-Turkish or Russo-Japanese wars. Even the Soviet invasion of Afghanistan, which had a direct effect on the families of various nationalities and left a number of young men from Latvia dead or maimed, seemed distant – and fought in some mythical faraway land. And the only reminder that it was real after all was the awareness that I too, once I reached the age of eighteen, would, in all likelihood, have been drafted and ended up in Afghanistan. Yet the war in Afghanistan ended and I celebrated my eighteenth birthday when the Soviet Army was still in Latvia, but Latvia's independence had been restored.

My mother and father are old enough to remember the war, whereas my generation and the one in between have only heard about it. In a way we too resemble the so-called "Generation Golf" that came of age during the prosperous 1980s in Western Europe, which the German journalist Florian Illies described, and which very closely resembled the generation which, after a long period of peace, flung itself into the misery and destruction of the First World War in 1914, like moths stunned by a light bulb. Even peace and relative prosperity can turn out to be a heavy and exhausting burden.

Thinking about all this has made me realise I never asked my parents about what they knew of their parents' experience of the First World War.

"My mother didn't talk about it," Father replied. "I don't know why. But I remember that my great uncle, her father's brother, said that during wartime, after he finished his coffee, he also ate the grounds – that's how hungry he was."

His father had been a rifleman who, after the revolution in Russia, wandered from Murmansk to Vladivostok and returned to Latvia only after its independent statehood was established.

My mother's father was born in Russia and their family also returned to Latvia after November 1918. A few years later, they took on the lease of the estate on the banks of Lake Ķīšezers, where my mother spent much of her childhood.

While we ate pastries and drank coffee, it turned dark outside. Christmas is little more than a month away, we said. The wind was icy at the crossroads in front of the theatre, and we walked across the esplanade to an alley of trees that moaned dismally, where I had the idea of taking a picture of my parents – with my mobile, for I don't even remember when I last touched a real camera. Even though the alley was dimly lit by street lights, I turned on the flash and took a couple of pictures. My mother was wiping away tears and said that it must have been the biting wind and the light had been so bright that her eyes would probably be closed in the picture. I saw them off at the station.

"Now we won't see each other for a long time," my mother said.

"Not that long," I objected.

"When will you come for a visit?" Father asked.

"Once we're back, I'll come right away," I promised.

We said our goodbyes. I hugged her and once again was struck by how gaunt she had become over the years, how frail and small. Such human contact was alien to my father and he just waved his hand, yet this behaviour must have been in conflict with what was happening in his soul, for I thought that I spotted tears in his eyes. He immediately turned and walked away. My mother followed him slowly after a pause, and I looked after them for quite some time.

19 November

The only thing I hate about such days is the early start. I'm only half there for the entire morning. The last things into the suitcase, the last half-drunk coffee, one last look into the bag to check whether my mobile phone charger, book, passport and tickets are there, and then the phone rings and the taxi is waiting downstairs by the door. It's still very dark, almost nothing can be picked out on either bank of the river; everything is covered in a thick, impenetrable fog. And the same kind of fog remains in my head until the moment that I've passed through all the security checks, had a glass of Prosecco at the airport café and finally collapsed into my seat on the plane. I know that I won't read the book now, in all likelihood won't when I reach my destination, and I won't read it on my way back, either. But it's nice to know it's there.

I had an acquaintance whose wife took him to the forest in the middle of a late autumn night and left him there in his pyjamas with a scratched face – thirty kilometres from Riga. It was just one episode in the drama of their separation and finally they did get a divorce. He married for a second time, and that too ended in a divorce, I believe, but it's his being taken into the forest that I keep thinking about. It seems to have something to do with ancient horrendous magic rituals, such as expelling criminals from the village, putting old people on sleds and abandoning them in the forest – the forest was seen as the opposite of order, civilisation and security.

Latvia is supposed to be one of the "greenest" countries in Europe. In spite of savage logging, most of our country is still covered by forests. This may be the reason why every year, once the dark autumn and winter months have set in, I get an irresistible urge to get away from the sight of wet and dripping spruces and the congealing ghost-time darkness amongst the trees. This is the season when I feel that the forest, with the weight it has sucked up from the earth, its mouldy stench and its depressing darkness, is poised to devour us.

And so it is nice to know that there's the little house in Majorca, which our friends bought many years ago and where we can pass this time of year. I remember how tears welled up in my eyes upon seeing wild palm trees for the first time. Of course, these too are trees, yet they have hardly anything in common with our spruces, pines, hazels, aspens and others. They were rooted in a completely different soil. For some reason, it made me happy and filled my heart with a pleasant lightness. I was no longer the person from the fogs of Riga, from our summers in the country meadow by the pond or from our autumns in the forest: I was not the same man people have got to know in our daily business, I was another. And yet I was myself. Now there were at least two I's. Or even more. I, I, I…

20 November
The idea of polite small talk with strangers sitting next to you was probably born at the time when air travel was still very expensive and a luxury available only to members of high society. Hellos, introductions, mutual politeness, enquiries as to the destination, finding out about common interests, perhaps even the beginning of a beautiful friendship – all of that was part of travel. Yet as the plane tickets have become ever cheaper and the flight conditions ever more democratic, the relationships between fellow travellers have also changed. People from all walks of life are forced to rub shoulders, and it would be wrong to suppose that the majority would have anything in common at all – except perhaps respect for the person next to them and the basic rules of hygiene.

I am also no longer interested in having casual conversations with my fellow travellers, particularly if the person sitting next to me turns out to be my compatriot. Even at the airport – whether leaving Riga or returning to it – I am overcome by a need to separate myself from the other Latvians and not reveal that I am one myself. I feel uncomfortable that I belong with them and feel embarrassed about everything – their looks, behaviour, overheard conversations, naivety, narrow-mindedness, lack of education and shallowness. I always feel relieved when the airport employees or stewardesses address me in their limited English, for they have taken me for someone else – someone I am not. At such moments, I feel like a secret agent who, after successfully changing his appearance, has launched upon another dangerous mission without a definite task and expected result, yet with an unshakeable faith that I always have a place to come back to – even if that means constant comings and goings.

Ending No. 1

The memory of my mobile phone was full, there was no space for new photographs, and last night, I finally sat down to sort the pictures and get rid of some. I had not done it for a couple of years and now, with curiosity as well as incomprehension, I looked at poorly lit pictures taken for unknown purposes and rediscovered places I'd ended up in but which I had soon forgotten. Now as I looked at the pictures, I remembered not only the scenes, but also the scents and sounds, and even whether it had been warm or cold, or whether there'd been strong wind or rain.

I remembered a damp and overcast day when I ended up in the over the spruce-cone-drying house near Smiltene, which had been built more than century before. A sizeable stove was lit in the smallish red-brick building, and the hot air rose from below, drying the cones in large wire baskets. The spruce cones opened in the warmth and the seeds that fell out were put in sacks. The whole building smelt of dry timber and resin. Of course I'd known that forests don't always seed themselves and that sometimes they are planted, yet I had never wondered how the seedlings are obtained. The drying house, originally built for a country estate, was the place where enormous man-made stretches of forest originated, then to be cut and regrown.

Nearby was a nursery where in Soviet times pines had been planted for harvesting seed pine cones. The gnarly pines grew in straight rows, with their crowns kept intentionally low. From the ravine behind the pine plantation a river was heard and on its bank, overgrown with thorny sweet briar, nettles and alder thickets, the baron's hunting lodge still stood. Its windows broken, Dutch tile stoves ruined and doors torn off their hinges, the large three-storey building still radiated self-confidence and strength.

Now something caught my eye in one of the pictures, which I had taken from the second-floor window of that building. At a maximum enlargement, it looked like someone was standing in the shadows on the edge of the forest. It is of course possible that it was simply the stump of a gnarled tree broken by the wind.

Then followed the pictures from the evening when my parents had come to Riga. They had not turned out. Two overexposed little figures were standing against a dramatically dark background. Mother and Father looked tiny and frightened, not to mention a passer-by had managed to insinuate himself into three of the four pictures. In the first, he was seen in the background to the right, in the second already almost at the centre, behind my parents' backs, and in the third, he had got to the left side of the picture, stopped and was staring back into the camera with two dark, shadowy sockets for eyes. The flash had barely touched him, his outline was very blurry. I pressed "delete" and got rid of the picture.

Ending No. 2

At the end of last August I went on a hike from Riga to Valga. I began walking early in the morning – past Lake Ķīšezers, then on the railway bridge across the Jugla, past Lake Baltezers, along the Gauja, to Murjāņi, and so on.

On my way, I tried to avoid the big highways – I preferred

to take a detour. During the day it was still sunny and warm, but at night it was chilly. I spent my nights wherever it was convenient – in a tent in the bushes by the roadside, with friends or at previously arranged lodgings. Five days later, I had reached my destination and, even though it seemed too fast, the experience of walking was mostly a surprise because of its absolutely non-contemporary speed. Walking kilometre after kilometre, entering townships or walking out of them it seemed that I was gradually achieving a different rhythm, divorced from the contemporary rush of time. That was the goal of my hike, for I had started entering into the computer the 1917–1918 diaries of an anonymous author. He wrote about himself that he could be "Someone but, even better, something", because at that time there were many like him.

I finished copying on the day when it became clear that Russia would not return Crimea to Ukraine. I leafed through the pages covered in neat and elegant handwriting that had fallen out of notebooks, and intermittently glanced at Internet news websites. It seemed unbelievable and yet it was reality – state borders and international agreements were unimportant. The feeling of peace and security could prove to be an illusion at the drop of the hat.

At the end of the summer of 1917, many Latvians left Riga and its environs. Any day, Riga could have been invaded by German troops, and the refugees travelling by cart or on foot sought shelter first in Valka and then in St Petersburg or even further east. Not even thirty years had passed and many again had to prepare for the road – this time in the opposite direction – and thus the phenomenon we still call "exile" was born.

Even as late as last autumn, walking in the direction of Valka, I had no idea that six months later people would think about or openly consider questions that in all likelihood also worried our ancestors during the first and second world wars. As the news from Ukraine and the Crimea grew ever more worrying, it would seem that anyone with any amount of imagination had to wonder what he or she would do under similar circumstances. Patriotic fighters from couches and social networks got involved in heated arguments with theoreticians of escape strategies about what Latvia's Armed Forces should be like and what they should be doing at the moment of an external (or externally "internal") aggression. There might have been more opinions expressed than there are soldiers in our army.

"Immediately into the car and off through Lithuania and Poland to the West," some said.

"Never! The land border will definitely be the first to be closed," others objected.

"Have to go through Belarus," still others fantasised.

"Boat's the only way! Have to keep a boat ready," was the wisdom of the fourth group that seemed to have forgotten how it ended for the legionnaires who managed to get to Sweden by boat.

"We must have an ample supply of canned goods and other necessities," was the opinion of the fifth group.

"No one should stay in the cities," was the wisdom of the sixth.

"Off to the forest!" tweeted the seventh group.

"… the average Latvian has a Schmeisser hidden under the eaves," the eighth declared recalling what they'd heard when they were children, even though they didn't know what a Schmeisser looked like.

"We have membership in the European Union and NATO," believed the ninth, though they remembered their parents' or grandparents' stories of waiting for the Americans after the Second World War.

"I don't know what I'd do," was what the tenth group said and they may have been right. No matter how reasonable, good or reliable each plan for fighting or survival might have seemed to the individual exponents, taken together they were all a reflection of human ignorance of uncontrollable chaos.

A while back, fighting a bout of boredom, I read somewhere that some of our memories may not be our own, but may instead be inherited from our ancestors congenitally – and not just from parents, but also from grandparents or even older generations. Researchers had discovered this through their experiments with rats. No, rats of course were not able to tell the story of the taste of the madeleines eaten by their ancestors, yet the reactions expressed during the experiment to certain impulses – tastes, smells, sounds – were somehow miraculously transferred from one generation to another and then to another. A minute ago, I heard on the radio that once again nineteen soldiers were dead and ninety-three wounded in Ukraine, whereas Israel was bombing the Gaza strip for a fourth consecutive day and the number of dead had reached one hundred.

Wars, revolutions, uncertainty about the future, fear of death, and death, suffering and horror everywhere, despair and loss of hope – these are experiences that are difficult to simply call impulses. I would not be surprised if the imprints and scars – akin to the embankments of lost railways, gardens of destroyed houses and overgrown roads – have reached us from our parents or grandparents without our awareness. Nor would I be surprised if they did not disappear long after we are gone.

Afterword

Eternal Resurrection

History

"It was a cold November night, the wind kept rattling the shop signboards, and a bitter chill penetrated my ragged coat," Aleksandrs Grīns (1895–1941) wrote in his story "Resurrection". "As the wind threw dry leaves at my feet, I started walking slowly along the canal path towards the citadel, but came to a halt by the former Russian theatre, where a strange flag was hanging over the balcony and billowing in the wind. Red-white-red, it darted about like a dark flickering flame, but none of the windows were lit, all the nearby streets were empty, and I didn't see anyone whom I could have asked what kind of a flag it was. And again, I felt a muted rustling sound closing in from the tree-lined side of the canal, and that was the whooshing of dry leaves being chased by a gush of wind or trampled by some-one concealed by the dark of the night. ... I sat down on the pavement by the theatre entrance to catch my breath and rest my tired feet and, following a new burst of moon-light, returned to observing the flag which was now flutter-ing right above my head, throwing a huge shadow into the small square in front of the theatre, and the shadow was reproducing the flapping of the flag. ... The cold, which made me draw deeper into my soldier's coat, seemed to be coming not from the ground or the air, but from the bulky giants shouldering the weight of the theatre balcony and, having glanced at them, I noticed someone in the shady doorway who stirred and then, with light, inaudible steps, started walking towards me. And I was gripped by new shudders of cold and also wonder, for the stranger cast no shadow, despite the fresh beam of moonlight, and he was bringing along the chill of the grave."

The scene depicted here takes place on 18 November 1918. It may be the dread instilled by this and other stories by Grīns, which I read as a child, that made me choose the moment of the birth of the Latvian state for the temporal setting of my novel.

Our assumptions about events of that autumn tend to differ radically from the atmosphere crafted by Grīns. We see the ceremonious, solemn founders of Latvia's statehood, the stage of the present-day National Theatre adorned with the lavish spread of the red-white-red flag and house-plants in Vilis Rīdzenieks's photograph and feel inclined to treat the events which preceded or followed it, or were not enclosed by the walls of this theatre, more as a preface to this moment, as chapters written before or after it, or as footnotes or an afterword.

Every year on 18 November, we unfold Latvian flags and hold official anniversary ceremonies; in families and circles of friends, less sombre and a good deal warmer festivities probably take place too. It's a small wonder that we celebrate this distant date marking the birth of the Latvian state with such a large festival. It seldom occurs to anyone that not many people would have been there to celebrate it back in 1918. We frequently ascribe expansiveness retrospectively to events and perceive some suggestive details only much later.

Imagine that autumn. The war was supposed to be over (an armistice between Germany and the entente was signed on 11 November), but it wasn't – the Treaty of Versailles was signed on 28 June 1919, but battles for the liberation of Latvia raged on in Latgale until the summer of 1920. Courland and Riga, on 18 November 1918, were under the

Germans. The year before, tens of thousands of refugees from Courland and Riga ventured ever further to the East, with quite a few ending up at the eastern borders of the Eurasian continent. Meanwhile, the Bolsheviks were pressing in from Russia. Amongst all this chaos, destruction, hopelessness and mortal danger, a small group of Latvians got together in the middle of an occupied city and founded their own national state, something which would have seemed impossible even a year earlier.

Almost a hundred years separate us from that moment, yet we keep returning to the question to which the men who climbed on to that stage on 18 November 1918 seemed to have had a clear answer: Why do we need a state of our own?

Memory

Although memory is an integral part of written history, this faculty, sense, or burden of ours is also extremely unreliable. What we fail to write down or tell others is easily forgotten, while we're often inclined to remember things we've never experienced but only heard or read somewhere.

We have access to factual accounts, synopses of speeches and journal entries, and historical works have emerged later along with a range of other kinds of material focusing on 18 November 1918 and the period preceding it. The theatre house is still where it always was and so are the streets, albeit under different names, and the city canal, Bastejkalns. Who knows, perhaps there are still a few of the same trees.

And yet to travel back through time and step into that very place is no longer in anyone's power. It is too late to search for those who witnessed the fact. An author intending to write about events in a past he has not experienced faces a difficult choice. Should I cheat and make people unknown to me express and do things which I may simply wish to have happened? Or would it be better to stick to documentary sources and leave aside such interesting things as stories, relationships between characters, feelings – in other words, everything that is typically expected from a novel?

The form of my novel is the result of such musings. I decided that it should be based on the uncertainty generated between the specifics of the present and those of the past. It is something well known to historians and archaeologists when faced with the need to decipher a fragment of text or make sense of some object once used for an undisclosed purpose. I decided that, in terms of genre, this would be a novel of ideas sans melodrama – all the romantic side plots shrivelled up and died early on.

In part, the tension results from the difference between the speed of the passage of time now and a hundred years ago. Although the telephone and telegraph had already been invented, there were zeppelins floating in and aeroplanes shooting across the sky, steamers ploughing the seas and steam-powered engines running on the railways, the world still remained very slow and vast, and its ends were at a great distance from one another.

In the era of television news and social media, it seems self-evident to us that a pile-up in Asia, a marketplace massacre in the Middle East or a robbery in rural Latvia may travel the globe minutes or even seconds after the event. Not to know is no longer considered a symptom of illiteracy or a sign of poor upbringing – now, ignorance begins to be seen as an attribute of a particularly refined or disciplined lifestyle.

It was different a century ago. Those leaving Courland or Riga in a hurry and heading eastwards as refugees found themselves out of touch with what was happening back home once they were a few dozen miles away from it, and the further they went from more highly populated areas, what awaited them ahead became less clear. Fear, suspicion, hope and rumours spread along the muddy or dusty dirt roads, across fields and forests quite like messages on the Internet today – only at a much slower pace. But speed is not an antidote for ignorance – if speed is our only aim, we'll be incapable of answering the great questions of our days.

Thus journal entries became for me the natural mode of expression in this novel: one of the diary writers is a witness to the events of 1917–1918 and the other is our contemporary. One lives in uncertainty and unpredictability not only of what the next day will bring, but quite often also of what is happening around him; the other one confronts ignorance, trying to grasp the evidence left by history and the way it relates to the reality of the present.

The diary is an exceptionally subjective form of self-expression; even authors, who may harbour some hope that one day their writings will be read by descendants or successors, feel they can be self-righteous in their journals, free from the need for objectivity, and yet remain tormented by uncertainty and end up with fallacies. Writing first of all for writing's sake, the author of a diary often unwittingly becomes an even less reliable narrator than all those untrustworthy storytellers, fantasists and liars whom writers so willing choose as the protagonists of their works.

Landscape

As a writer, I like to challenge myself with tasks that may seem hopeless at first. I have been conflicted about (not to say repulsed by) the descriptions of nature in literary works ever since the mandatory reading lists we were given at school. I know I'm not alone in this, yet my aversion to such adulatory prose regarding nature may be exceptionally violent, since it is precisely for this reason that I can never share the enthusiasm for J.R.R. Tolkien's The Lord of the Rings (I hope his many fans will forgive me).

This time I decided to get over this quirk of mine, so various natural phenomena have been accorded quite a significant space in the novel. Nevertheless, this element is not an end in itself and, as one of my characters might say, I haven't done it just for the hell of it.

Although populated, cultivated, ruined and transformed, the basic scenery of Latvia is considerably more ancient than we are, whichever generation we belong to, and in all likelihood, it must have influenced us much more deeply than the other way round. In a sense, our landscape is akin to our language, for we were not the ones who created it, whatever assumptions we may have. Nor is it our possession. Resulting from chains of random coincidence, it has been allotted for our use for a brief stretch of time. And the only thing we can and should do is to try not to mess it up too badly or lose it all together.

Since one part of the events I describe herein was remote and out of reach, it was important for me to balance this lack of knowledge with something solid, something available to my senses, something I know and have been acquainted with. For that reason, all the landscapes described in the novel are – as much as possible – real and can be found on a map. What they reflect is based on my observations or on other people's oral or written accounts.

Latvia is a relatively small country; even the furthermost border points of our land are not all that distant from each other. I proved it to myself by undertaking a few days' hike from Riga to Valka. In my attempt to encompass the entire territory of the state founded on 18 November 1918, I counterbalanced the stream of refugees headed for Valka, described in the novel, with the westward movement of people away from Riga – to the Liv-populated villages in Courland. I have been fortunate to spend a good deal of time in Miķeļtornis, where a considerable part of this novel was written, so it's almost natural that it turned out to be the location of the first impossible encounter between the two protagonists separated by time.

What is eaten and how it's eaten have always been very

important in Latvian everyday life. In the novel, mentions of particular dishes and drinks have not been incidental or anachronistic dues paid to the ubiquitous Internet postings about people's eating adventures and snapshots of food. I always remember the story of a relative living abroad and visiting Latvia in the 1960s and how impressed he had been by the culinary talents of the locals and their eagerness to surprise their guests with food. Only the very best food to be found had been spread on the table, and it seems that this tradition – to treat guests to choice foods even in poor or dire circumstances – reveals some primeval and by now totally mystifying deeper understanding. It is difficult to say whether or not our tradition of feeding the souls of our deceased (*veļi*) derives from this wisdom or, on the contrary, the spirits of the dead were once perceived simply as visitors from particularly remote realms.

I am writing this in the evening of 23 August, the twenty-fifth anniversary of the Baltic Way, which was held in 1989. All day long, memories of participants of that event, live reports from the memorial events in Latvia and those taking place in neighbouring Lithuania and Estonia have been aired on the TV and radio. I was sixteen at the time and had just passed my entrance exams to the Riga School of Applied Arts; within a week, our classes were to begin in Riga, to be preceded by a mandatory journey to do some beetroot harvesting in one of the collective farms in Salaspils. The state collective farm was still firmly in its place, but I wished to get a badge in the form of the Latvian symbol for the morning star (*auseklītis*) and attach it to my nylon windbreaker. It was a sizeable enamelled badge, in all likelihood secretly produced in the Daiļrade handicraft shops and, having launched the production of this coveted attribute of the Awakening, someone had already jumped on the bandwagon of consumerism. "You know, if you are caught by Russians wearing this thing, they'll make you swallow it," I was told by one of my new study buddies.

History is not some past endangered by forgetting. It is what remains within every one of us, as well as in our landscape and language.

"Today, they'll announce the resurrection of Latvia in this building; this here is its flag, and our brothers fallen in the bog of Tīreļpurvs will rise from their graves and join the battle if the living hesitate to help their homeland," the ghost says to Grīns's protagonist during their encounter outside the theatre. "This voice faded in a rustle of leaves, the speaker obliterated by moonlight and the billowing banner, and I continued on my way to search for the place where I could sign up as a volunteer, ready to go and help the land of my fathers again, this time around, as its own soldier. And the rustle of dry leaves, whispering with the voices of my friends fallen in battle, kept me company that night."

Miķeļtornis, 23 August 2014

Acknowledgements

I would not have been able to imagine or write this story by myself. I would not have been able to do it without my family, without my mother and father and all my departed forebears. I would not have been able to write it without those places in Latvia that are important and dear to me and without all of the trees, shrubs, usable and overgrown roads, waterways or simple hillocks that never cease to address me in their own special way and call me to them. Many of the people, events and scenes described are figments of my imagination, yet many historic facts and details I have borrowed from the writings of other authors or the life stories of people unknown to me, yet nevertheless real.

A special thanks to Alda Staprāns-Mednis who introduced me to the memoir of Sergejs Staprāns, *Through the Darkness of Russia to the Latvian Sun*, for it was Sergejs's temperament, adventurer's nature and experiences that in a way inspired this story.

As I wrote, I often felt the need to consult Mariss Vētra's book *Riga Then: A Memoir*, Anna Brigadere's memoir about 1917–1918 entitled *The Iron Fist*, the seemingly inexhaustible volume by Ādolfs Šilde, *History of Latvia, 1914-1940*, Marija Šuvcāne's book *The Liv Village that Is No More*, and the Latvian press archives on the website www.periodika.lv of the Latvian National Library. Likewise, I surely was affected by the ghosts of riflemen that I encountered as a child in stories by Aleksandrs Grīns, *Coup de Grâce* by Marguerite Yourcenar and the Volker Schlöndorff film based on it. With some of the